GABRIEL'S HONOR

BARBARA McCAULEY

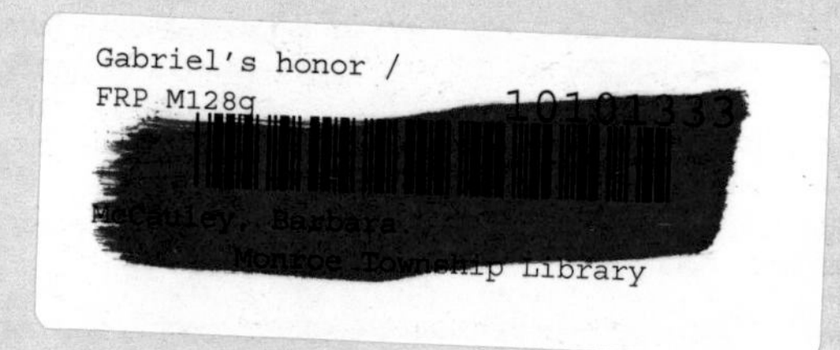

Published by Silhouette Books
America's Publisher of Contemporary Romance

To my husband, Frank—I love you.

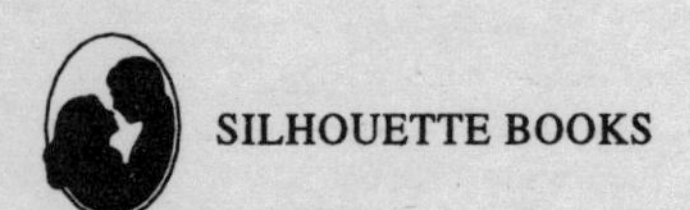

ISBN 0-373-27094-1

GABRIEL'S HONOR

This edition published by arrangement with Harlequin Books S.A.

Visit Silhouette at www.eHarlequin.com

Printed in U.S.A.

Books by Barbara McCauley

Silhouette Intimate Moments

†*Gabriel's Honor* #1024

†Secrets!
*Hearts of Stone

Silhouette Desire

Woman Tamer #621
Man From Cougar Pass #698
Her Kind of Man #771
Whitehorn's Woman #803
A Man Like Cade #832
Nightfire #875
**Texas Heat* #917
**Texas Temptation* #948
**Texas Pride* #971
Midnight Bride #1028
The Nanny and the Reluctant Rancher #1066
Courtship in Granite Ridge #1128
Seduction of the Reluctant Bride #1144
†*Blackhawk's Sweet Revenge* #1230
†*Secret Baby Santos* #1236
†*Killian's Passion* #1242
†*Callan's Proposition* #1290

BARBARA McCAULEY

was born and raised in California and has spent a good portion of her life exploring the mountains, beaches and deserts so abundant there. The youngest of five children, she grew up in a small house, and her only chance for a moment alone was to sneak into the backyard with a book and quietly hide away.

With two children of her own now and a busy household, she still finds herself slipping away to enjoy a good novel. A daydreamer and incurable romantic, she says writing has fulfilled her most incredible dream of all—breathing life into the people in her mind and making them real. She has one loud and demanding Amazon parrot named Fred and a German shepherd named Max. When she can manage the time, she loves to sink her hands into fresh-turned soil and make things grow.

Chapter 1

The Victorian farmhouse sat quietly in the darkness at the end of the quarter-mile-long gravel driveway. The house was two-story, Cape Cod blue, though the clapboard siding hadn't seen the wet end of a paintbrush for at least twenty years. A chill touched the night air like an icy hand; light from a half-moon shone down on the roof, which was missing more shingles than a professional hockey team was missing front teeth. The porch steps were a broken leg waiting to happen, and tall, spiky weeds choked what might have once been daisies in the dried-up front flower bed.

Gabriel Sinclair stood on the porch of the old house and frowned at the locked front door. It had been a long time since he'd broken into a house. Fifteen years, to be exact. He'd been twenty years old at the time, on a clandestine mission with his three younger brothers. Gabe had been appointed lookout while Callan waited in the getaway truck; Reese, the youngest at fifteen, found the open window, and Lucian, the most daring Sinclair—and only seventeen at the time—slipped inside Lucy Greenwood's bedroom window and snatched a pair of her hot pink satin underwear.

By the end of that night, all eight Bloomfield County High School cheerleaders had found themselves minus one pair of panties. The Sinclair brothers were brought into the sheriff's station and questioned, but later released due to lack of evidence. There'd been no proof, but everyone in town knew that the Sinclair boys were to blame. Who else would have even attempted—let alone pulled off—such a nefarious plan?

He smiled. Those were the days.

Gabe's smile slowly faded as he remembered the lecture that his parents had given all four of their sons that night. What he wouldn't give to hear one of those lectures now, Gabe thought. To see his father grim-faced and stern, dragging his callused carpenter's hand through his coal-black hair while he paced back and forth in front of his sons, and his mother standing quietly by, shaking her pretty blond head.

Damn, but he missed them. Missed his mother's soft laugh and her warm chocolate-chip cookies. Missed his father's quiet nod of approval for a job well-done, hot Sunday afternoons and a family game of horseshoes in the backyard.

With a heavy sigh, Gabe turned his attention back to the problem at hand: finding a way into the house.

He jiggled the tarnished brass front doorknob one more time, but it was definitely locked tight and dead bolted. He let the rusted screen door squeak loudly shut, then moved to the front windows. They were latched, as well.

Damn.

I'll leave the front door open, his sister, Cara, had told him earlier. *If you can work up a rough list of necessary repairs and meet me at the tavern tonight, I'll make dinner next Sunday, your choice.*

Since most of Gabe's bachelor-pad dinners were takeout, microwaved or sandwiches from his brother Reese's tavern in town, the idea of a home-cooked meal was entirely too tempting to pass up. His mouth was already watering from the menu he'd picked out: A big, juicy roast, fluffy mashed potatoes smothered in butter and hot gravy, melt-in-your-mouth biscuits like their mom used to make every Sunday. And then Cara's supreme specialty—apple pie.

Inspired by the image of food, Gabe hurried around to the back of the house, made a mental note to check the overhead door on the detached garage. He didn't even think that Mildred Witherspoon—the home's now deceased owner—had a car, so Gabe assumed that the garage door would also be in need of maintenance.

Behind the garage, cornfields leased out and tended by a neighboring farmer rustled in the chilly night breeze, and Gabe paused for a moment to listen to the calming sound. He and his brothers had played in the cornfields by their house when they were kids; hide-and-seek, soldier, cowboys and Indians. When he was twelve, he'd kissed Linda Green in those cornfields. Linda was married with three kids now.

Smiling, Gabe shook his head at the memory, then jumped up the steps of the back porch and tried the door. It was locked, as well. And dead bolted.

So were all the windows on the bottom floor.

Strange.

Gabe frowned. Mildred Witherspoon certainly had believed in sturdy locks. Which was odd, because very few people in Bloomfield County ever locked their doors. Crime was practically nonexistent in the quiet town, unless you counted jaywalking or an occasional speeding ticket on the open highway crime.

Or panty-raids, Gabe thought with a smile.

But Mildred would definitely have been safe from *that* infraction of the law. She'd been ninety-two when she quietly passed away in her sleep two weeks ago. A stoic, straitlaced woman whose manner was as Victorian as her house. When Mildred's lawyer had read her will, it had been a surprise to everyone when they learned that the elderly woman had left her farmhouse and all of its contents to the Killian Shawnessy Foundation, an organization to help women in need. Cara was vice president of the foundation, her husband, Killian Shawnessy, was president.

The funds from the sale of the house and its contents would be well-used by the organization. Gabe had already promised a donation of labor from Sinclair Construction, the now five-year-old construction company that he and Callan and Lucian were partners in, but Cara needed some figures ASAP on the cost of materials for repairs.

So here he was, standing in the dark, hands in his pockets, locked out.

He looked up at the second-story windows.

The Sinclairs never gave up without a fight. They thrived on challenges, laughed in the face of adversity. And we're talking apple pie here, folks, Gabe thought with a fresh burst of determination. Cara's apple pie was definitely worth a few scrapes and bruises.

Muttering curses, Gabe climbed the front porch railing, held his breath at the crack of wood, then grabbed hold of the edge of the porch roof. With a grunt, he pulled himself up and crawled carefully to a second-story window where he yanked on the weathered screen. It held tight. He yanked harder. When it came loose, it slammed into his face and sliced across his cheek. He swore hotly and tossed the screen aside, then reached for the window.

It was open.

With a shout of male victory, he climbed through the open window into what appeared to be a large bedroom. In the darkness, he could almost make out a four-poster bed and a nightstand with a lamp on it. The room was musty, but Gabe also caught the faint scent of something feminine and floral. Probably sachet or potpourri, he thought, though this scent was much more pleasant than the frilly lace balls that Sheila Harper, his last girlfriend, had tucked into every drawer and closet of her house. When she'd asked him to move in with her, all he could think about was his shirts and socks smelling like a damn perfume counter. Knowing that Sheila was looking for much more than a roommate, Gabe had cooled that relationship faster than she could say "wedding ring."

Not that he was against marriage. As long as it was someone else who did the marrying. His brother Callan had recently succumbed to the institution of matrimony, and his sister, Cara, had also gotten married a few months before Callan. The family was steadily growing, and he had no doubt that soon they'd be hearing the patter of little feet.

But Gabe was perfectly content with his life just as it was: single, no complications. Free as a bird. Socks and T-shirts that smelled like detergent, not flowers, thank you very much. And he was also content for the patter of little feet to be nieces and nephews. In fact, he looked forward to it.

He was reaching for the lamp's switch when he heard the squeak of floorboards in the hallway outside the bedroom. He froze, then slowly turned toward the door and listened.

Footsteps?

The house was quiet around him; the only sound was the hoot of an owl from the trees outside. He waited, but there was only silence. Shaking his head, he turned back to the lamp.

And stopped.

There it was again. Not as loud as before, but he heard it clearly—the unmistakable creak of a wood floor. Then another.

The house was supposed to be empty. Mildred Witherspoon had lived alone, she'd had no children and had never been married. Her lawyer had searched for family members following the reading of the will, just in case some long-lost nephew or cousin had suddenly turned up, crying their eyes out over poor old Aunt Mildred, who they were certain wanted to leave them all her earthly possessions.

But the search had turned up nothing, and it seemed that Miss Witherspoon had indeed been completely alone. Which meant that if someone was in the house, they most certainly didn't belong here.

He moved soundlessly toward the closed bedroom door, opened it carefully.

Squeak. Quiet. *Squeak.* Quiet.

They moved slowly down the stairs.

"Whoever you are," Gabe said firmly, and his voice echoed in the house, "stop right where you are."

The house went absolutely still, as if it had stopped breathing. Then the footsteps resumed, only this time at a run.

Dammit.

Gabe dashed into the dark hallway, made out the dim outline of the stairs to the left and ran toward them. He reached the top of the landing at the same instant his quarry hit the bottom. Gabe barely caught a glimpse of the intruder before he disappeared around the corner.

"Dammit, stop!"

Stumbling and cursing, he took the stairs three at a time, hit the bottom and rounded the corner into the dining room.

And stopped short when a fist slammed into his gut.

The punch lacked power, but the surprise took his breath away. His assailant had already turned and was running away when Gabe leaped after him and caught his legs in a flying tackle. They both went facedown on the hardwood floor in a tangle of arms and legs. A dining-room chair turned over and landed with a crash in the dark room, then a small table went on its side and the clatter of metal on wood rang out.

When an elbow smashed into Gabe's nose, he swore fiercely, then wrestled his attacker's arms behind his back and pinned them there. There was plenty of fight, but no bulk to the guy, no muscle, and he was considerably shorter than Gabe's own six-four frame. A teenager? he wondered and shifted his weight so he wouldn't hurt the kid.

"Let go of me!"

Gabe went still at the sound of the furious, but distinctly feminine voice.

A woman?

She squirmed underneath him, and with him lying on top of her, her rounded bottom wiggled against his lower regions.

Oh, yes, definitely a woman.

Her legs were long, he realized, her body and arms slender, but firm. And though it was subtle, she smelled like a spring bouquet. The same scent he'd caught a whiff of upstairs.

"I said, *let go of me.*" She spit each word out with such venom, Gabe was surprised he didn't see sparks fly with every syllable.

She started to struggle again, but he held her arms tightly, as much to protect himself against another elbow in his face as to give them both a moment to calm down.

"As soon as you relax," he said, and she countered with a quick thrust of her body that almost knocked him sideways. When he tightened the pressure on her wrists—small, delicate wrists, he noted—she sucked in a sharp, deep breath, then went still, her breathing heavy and strained.

"That's a good girl," he said, easing his hold on her. "Okay, I'm going to let you up now, slowly. I don't want to hurt you, but—"

"Please don't hurt my mommy."

Gabe froze at the sound of the tiny, frightened voice that came from a dark corner of the dining room. He felt the breath shudder out from the woman underneath him, heard her small choked-back sob.

A woman and a child? Hiding in the darkness in an empty house? What the hell was going on?

"I'm not going to hurt your mommy," Gabe said softly to the child as he released the woman. "She just surprised me, that's all."

He stood, then reached down and took hold of her arm to help her up, but she shook off his touch and moved quickly into the shadowed corner of the room to join the small figure huddled there.

"It's all right, baby," Gabe heard her say. "I'm fine. Don't worry."

They stood there, all three of them, without speaking, letting the darkness smooth a quiet hand over the tension. Gabe drew in a deep breath, then slowly let it out. "I'm going to turn on a light now. Are you going to run again?"

A long pause. "No."

He didn't believe her for an instant. He kept his gaze on the shadows as he ran his hand along the wall by the doorway, found the switch and flipped it on.

Light from a crystal chandelier poured into the room, but it still seemed dark. Dark wood paneling, dark green drapes, cherry wood dining-room table and buffet. The room had all the cheerfulness of a cave.

Wearing a long-sleeved, black turtleneck sweater and black jeans, and with hair the deep brown color of sable, the woman would have completely blended into the shadows of the room if not for her pale face and wide, thickly lashed eyes. For one brief moment, his gaze rested on her lips: wide, curved, slightly parted.

Damn, he thought, then quickly shook off the twist in his gut.

She stood in the corner, her shoulders stiff and straight, with her child behind her. He guessed her age to be somewhere in her mid-to-late-twenties. Her wary gaze lifted to his and held, and he could see that she indeed wanted to run, was merely waiting for the opportunity.

He moved between the two doorways in the room, effectively blocking her, but carefully keeping his distance.

"Who are you?" she demanded suddenly, catching him off guard. "What are you doing here?"

Gabe lifted one dark brow. "Funny, that's what I was just going to ask you."

"I'm a friend of Miss Witherspoon's." Her chin went up. "She was expecting my son and me."

Gabe glanced down and watched a sandy-blond head peek out from behind the woman's legs. Short, stubby fingers clutched tightly onto her slender thighs. Four or five, Gabe guessed the kid's age.

Gabe looked back at the woman. "I didn't see a car out front."

"I parked it in the garage out back," she said, placing a hand on the side of her son's head. "I needed the overhead light to unload."

Maybe, Gabe thought. Maybe not. He looked back up at the woman. "When?"

Her brow furrowed. "When what?"

"When was Miss Witherspoon expecting you?"

"Oh." She blinked quickly. "Well, actually, we weren't due to arrive until Friday, but I didn't think she'd mind if we were a couple of days early. It seems, however, that she's away at the moment."

That was an understatement, Gabe thought.

"I didn't think she'd mind if we waited for her," she added. "The last time we spoke, she was looking forward to our arrival."

The woman's voice was smooth, Gabe noted, with rich, deep tones, still a little breathless from their scuffling. "When did you speak with Miss Witherspoon last?" he asked.

"When did I speak with her?" she repeated hesitantly. "I'm not sure. Several days ago. Maybe last Tuesday or Wednesday. But I really don't see what business that is of yours."

"And that was last week, you say?"

"Give or take a day or two." Her eyes flashed as she shook her thick, dark hair away from her face. "Look, I don't appreciate your attitude. My son and I are invited guests here, and you're the one who broke in and frightened us half to death."

There was some truth in the woman's words, Gabe believed. But there were lies, as well. Especially the part about speaking with Miss Witherspoon the previous week. That would have been quite a conversation, considering she'd died two weeks ago.

But anyone who knew Mildred Witherspoon, also knew that the woman had never, in the ninety-two years she'd lived in the town, ever, invited anyone into her home. Other than the monthly meetings and Sunday services she attended, Mildred had tucked herself away as tightly as the bun on top of her head.

Which most certainly meant that the woman standing ten feet away from him was lying through her pretty white teeth.

"Look, mister, it's been a long day." The strain was apparent in the woman's thin voice and the tight press of her lips. "My son and I are tired. If Miss Witherspoon is out of town, then I'll just leave her a note and we'll be on our way in the morning."

He supposed he could just let it go, let her stay here with her child without questioning her. He seriously doubted that she'd come here to steal anything, or that Mildred Witherspoon even had anything worth stealing. What did he care if this woman stayed here and was on her way in the morning? Who was he to begrudge her a night's stay in an empty house?

But there was something in her eyes, something beyond the wary defiance. Something as quiet as it was fierce. Something desperate. And whatever that something was, it closed around him like a fist and squeezed.

Dammit, Gabe, just walk away.

Lord knew he didn't need or want any complications in his life. He should just do what he came here to do, then turn around, walk out the front door and go to Reese's tavern where he could toss back a beer or two. Not think about the frightened look in this woman's eyes. She'd be gone in the morning, and they could both forget they'd ever seen each other.

That's what he should do.

But he couldn't, dammit. He didn't know why, but he couldn't.

"Miss Witherspoon died two weeks ago," he said evenly. "Now do you want to try it again and tell me who you are and what you're doing here?"

Her breathing seemed to stop, and her eyes closed with what appeared to be genuine concern. She drew in a slow, shaky breath, then opened her eyes again.

"How?" she asked quietly.

"She just went to sleep and didn't wake up," Gabe replied. "We should all be so lucky at ninety-two."

"She seemed so much younger on the phone," the woman said thoughtfully. "So full of life."

"That's one way to describe her," Gabe replied. He could think of several other descriptions he'd keep to himself.

"I'm sorry about Miss Witherspoon," the woman said abruptly, then straightened her shoulders. "And since it now appears that we're imposing, my son and I will be on our way."

She reached behind her, took her son's small hand in her own and started for the doorway leading to the kitchen. "Come on, sweetie, we're going to leave now."

Gabe blocked her way. "You haven't told me who you are."

"I don't believe that's any of your business," she said coolly and tried to step around him.

He stepped in front of her again.

Her eyes narrowed with anger. Gabe stood close enough to the woman now to see that her eyes were gray. Dove-gray, with a dark charcoal ring around the iris.

When he pulled out the slim cell phone tucked into the back pocket of his jeans, he watched that soft gray harden to the color of steel.

"Get out of my way," she said tightly.

"I'm afraid not." He punched the buttons on his phone. "And since you won't talk to me, then we'll just have to call someone you will talk to." He pushed the Send button.

"No." She stared at the phone, her eyes suddenly wide with fear. "Please don't call the police. Please."

"I'm out at the Witherspoon house," Gabe said into the phone a moment later. "Get over here as soon as you can. Bring two of Reese's best." He paused, then said, "Yeah, I'll explain when you get here."

Gabe hung up the phone, watched the fear on the woman's face turn to panic as she gauged the distance to the opposite doorway. Even without a small child, she never would have made it. When her gaze swung back to his, the look of defeat in her eyes stabbed sharply into his gut.

She didn't want his help, that was for certain, Gabe thought with a sigh, but she sure as hell was going to get it.

Trapped.

Her heart pounding, Melanie Hart stared at her captor and fought back the dread welling up in her stomach. He was much too tall for her to outrun; those long legs of his could easily overtake her. And she'd already experienced firsthand the power and strength of his well-honed body, a body she would have greatly admired under different circumstances. He was solid muscle under his faded blue jeans and chambray shirt.

But she couldn't let herself be caught. Couldn't let the police find her and Kevin.

She took a step toward the doorway again, but the man moved with her, slowly shaking his head.

How could she fight him? Especially with Kevin clutching so tightly to her legs. Determination glinted in the man's dark green gaze, and the stubborn set of his strong jaw gave her no hope. The sight of blood on his angled cheek startled her. Had she done that in their scuffle? Guilt tugged at her, but she quickly shrugged it off. She hadn't meant to hurt him, but if necessary, she would. What choice did she have?

Lifting her chin, she drew in a slow breath to steady her nerves. "This is kidnapping," she said with a calm that amazed herself. "You have no reason, and certainly no right, to keep me and my son here. I want you to know I intend to press charges."

"Fair enough." He lifted a dark brow, then gestured toward the doorway leading to the living room. "In the meantime, why don't we go sit down? Filling out all those forms will be tiring."

Once again she thought about running, but the futility of escape loomed as dark as the night. She'd have to find some way to distract this man, or perhaps reason with him, though that possibility appeared to lie somewhere between slim and none.

He stayed close behind as she moved out of the dining room with her son, effectively squelching any ideas she might have had about dashing out the front door as they passed through the entry at the bottom of the stairs. When they stepped into the living room, he flipped on a small brass table lamp.

The room was spacious, high beveled ceilings, tall windows, hardwood floors. A fireplace big enough to drive a Volkswagen into. Oil paintings, mostly landscapes, hung on off-white walls. Two Queen Anne chairs and a long sofa were slip-covered, tables and desks and chairs of various styles and woods completed the room. Like the rest of the house, the scent was musty and stale.

Her captor gestured for her to sit. She glared at him, then took her son's hand and moved to the sofa.

How could she have known that Miss Witherspoon had died? She *had* spoken with the woman, though it had been four weeks ago, not last week. Melanie had known that the woman was elderly, but she'd sounded so fit, with too much grit and pluck to die. When she'd driven up a little while ago and discovered the house empty, Melanie had simply thought that the woman was away.

She knew that she'd made a mistake lying about Miss Witherspoon inviting her here, a big mistake. *Dammit.* She blinked back the threatening tears. She couldn't afford to make mistakes.

But she was tired. So incredibly tired. And so was Kevin. After leaving California, she'd taken her time zigzagging across the country. But the trip was taking its toll on both her and Kevin, not only the traveling and moving around, but the constant worry, the fear, was mentally exhausting.

But she couldn't stay here, especially now, with the police coming. She had no criminal record, but if she was charged with breaking and entering, then she would have one. And that might leave a trail she couldn't afford to leave. "Look, mister—"

"Gabe." He sat down on the arm of a Queen Anne chair. "Gabe Sinclair."

Melanie pulled her son onto her lap. His arms came around her neck as he attempted to burrow his cheek into her chest. She brushed her lips over his mop of soft hair and rocked him. "Mr. Sinclair, you're making a terrible mistake. My husband is an important man in Washington. He'll be furious that you kept me here without any cause or—"

"Call him." Gabe pulled his cell phone from his back pocket. "I'd like to speak with him."

"It's impossible to reach him right now." She

knew that she was digging her well of lies deeper and deeper. At this point, it hardly seemed to matter.

"You know," Gabe said, dragging a hand through his thick, dark hair, "you should at least wear a wedding ring if you're going to lie about being married, especially to a so-called important man. Why don't you just relax? It shouldn't be more than a few minutes."

Melanie sank back into the firm cushions of the sofa. She heard her son's stomach rumble and though he hadn't complained, she knew he was hungry. She'd been looking for something in the kitchen cupboards when she'd heard the truck pull into the gravel driveway, then seen a man approach the house. She'd barely had enough time to lock the front and back doors, hoping that he'd go away.

But after six weeks of sleeping in thin-walled, rundown motels, eating fast food and avoiding contact with people, it seemed as though her luck, along with most of her money, had finally run out.

And she had Mr. Gabe Sinclair to thank for that.

If not for him, she would have found food for her son and herself, gotten a good night's sleep here, and been fresh enough in the morning to drive to Raina's tomorrow. She'd be safe in Boston, at least for a few days.

Melanie glanced at the man sitting no more than eight feet from her. Arms folded across his wide chest, long legs stretched out, he watched her. She met his intense gaze, did not look away. She refused to be intimidated by him, even if he did have the upper hand.

Damn you, Gabe Sinclair, whoever the hell you are.

As if he'd read her thought, the man's eyebrows lifted slightly.

When Kevin stirred in her arms, Melanie turned her attention to her son and laid him on the sofa beside her. He curled up like a pill bug, tucking his small hands under his cheek and closing his eyes. Her heart swelled at the sight of him, and in spite of the odds, she resolved that she would get them safely out of this situation.

The only question that remained was, how?

When the light from an approaching car flashed brightly through the front windows and swept the room, her heart slammed against her ribs. The man glanced up, then rose.

It had to be now.

She scanned the room, and her gaze fell on a statue sitting on a table beside the sofa, a lovely, foot-tall bronze of an angel praying. Under normal conditions, Melanie would never have considered what she was considering. But this situation was as far from normal as one could get.

With his attention on the front door, the man moved past her and started across the room.

Now or never.

In one fluid movement, Melanie grabbed the statue and rushed the man, swinging the heavy bronze at his head. With an oath, he ducked, then reached out and plucked the statue from her as he grabbed her firmly around the waist. He dragged her to the door with him. She struggled wildly, but other than a wince when the heel of her boot connected with his shin and a rather explicit swearword, he ignored her.

When he let go of her with one hand while he unlocked the front door, she wiggled free and took off at a run. He had his long, muscled arms around her waist again in less than a heartbeat and easily lifted her off the ground.

"Gabriel Sinclair!" A woman's voice boomed. "Get your hands off that woman this instant!"

Chapter 2

Gabe turned sharply at the sound of his sister's voice. The wildcat woman in his arms went still.

Cara stood in the doorway, a hand on one hip, a large brown paper bag balanced on the other. The heavenly scent of grilled hamburgers and hot, crispy fries filled the room.

"For God's sake, Gabe, let her go," Cara repeated sharply.

Gabe set the woman down and released her. She stepped quickly away, dragging one shaky hand through her tousled hair, glancing from him to his sister.

The confusion on Cara's face turned quickly to an astute understanding that he had called her here for help. If anyone could help this renegade woman, Gabe absolutely knew his sister could.

"I apologize for Gabe's lack of manners," Cara said smoothly in a soft, calming voice. She snapped her gaze back to his and narrowed piercing blue eyes at him. "Shame on you."

Shame on *him?* Gabe ground his teeth and swore silently. He'd been kicked and scratched, and his left shin hurt like a son of a bitch. Females, he thought bitterly. Who would ever understand them?

With a toss of her blond head, Cara turned her attention back to the other woman and smiled. "I'm Cara Shawnessy," she said evenly. "This ape here is my brother."

Ape? He pressed his lips into a thin line. Gee, thanks, sis.

At the sound of a small whimper from the living room, the woman turned, then hurried back to her son. Cara glanced at Gabe, her gaze questioning, but he simply shrugged and shook his head.

Gabe held back when Cara moved into the living room and stood beside the sofa. "Would it be all right if we sat down and talked while we ate? I hope you like cheeseburgers and fries."

The woman gathered her son in her arms, and the glimmer of tears Gabe saw in her eyes caught like sawdust in his throat. He knew she wanted to refuse, he could see it in her hesitation, but when she looked at the bag of food in Cara's hand, then back at her son, she let out a long, surrendering breath and nodded. "That's very kind of you."

"It's the least I can do, especially after the way my brother manhandled you." Cara ignored the rude sound that Gabe made and smiled at the woman's young son, who was wide-awake now and watching all the adults around him. "Do you like pickles?" she asked the child.

The boy stuck a stubby finger into his mouth and

nodded shyly. Cara unwrapped a thick quarter slice and offered it to him. He hesitated, then looked at his mother. Smiling, she smoothed one slender hand over his rumpled blond hair. "It's all right, sweetheart. You can have it."

Eyes bright, he took the crisp pickle and bit in, chewing around a mumbled "thank you."

When a drop of juice fell onto the boy's pale blue T-shirt, Cara handed his mother some napkins. "It's optional," Cara said gently, "but it would be easier if you told me your names."

Gabe watched the woman's hand tighten around the napkins, saw the instinctive stiffening of her slender shoulders.

"You're safe here," Cara assured her. "You and your son."

Gabe saw the distrust in the woman's face when she glanced over at him. He frowned, unreasonably irritated that she obviously thought him a threat. She stared at him, her soft gray eyes uncertain and a little bit afraid. Damn if those eyes of hers didn't cut right through to his gut.

"Melanie," she whispered, still looking at him. "My son is Kevin."

Kevin sunk his teeth into another bite of pickle. "I'm four years old," he offered.

It drove Gabe nuts, but Cara didn't ask any questions, just chattered on about the weather as she unwrapped food and set everything out on the coffee table, including two sodas. She'd known to bring the hamburgers and fries when he'd asked for two of Reese's best, but she'd thrown the drinks in on her own.

"Gabe, I'm going to need that report for my board meeting in the morning." She pulled a thick paper cup of steaming black coffee out of her bag of tricks and brought it to him. "Will you be able to work up something rough for me in the next hour?"

His sister was kicking him out of here, he realized with a start. She didn't want him around while she talked to the woman. He ground his back teeth. *Damn you, Cara.* He didn't want to leave. He wanted to know what the hell was going on. Felt that he had some small right to at least a little information.

But Cara's expression was firm and definitely told him to get the hell out.

He frowned at her. "Sure. I'll, ah, just start in the kitchen. Check out the pipes and electricity."

"Thanks."

The single word was a dismissal. He glanced back at the woman—Melanie—felt her gaze follow him until he left the room.

He threw himself completely into his inspection, forced himself to think about wiring and water pressure instead of the woman with the sad, haunted look in her pale gray eyes.

Forty-five minutes later, Gabe leaned against the peeling white paint of a front porch column of the old house, gnawing impatiently on the end of an "It's a Boy" cigar. Six months ago, Wayne Thompson, the proud papa, had handed them out to every male over eighteen in Bloomfield County. Gabe had put the cigar in the glove box of his truck and nearly forgotten about it, but needing something to occupy his mind and hands for the past few minutes, he'd rooted around inside his truck until he'd found the stogie, then lit it up.

He decided that smoking a handful of stinkweed

would hold more appeal than Wayne's six-month-old cigar.

Spitting a piece of stale, harsh tobacco from the tip of his tongue, he stared at the front door. Cara had been in there with the woman and her son for almost an hour now, and though he'd heard their soft murmurs as he'd passed through the house, they'd all but forgotten his existence.

Hey, sis, remember me? The one who called you? I'm waitin' out here.

Frowning, he flicked an ash over the porch railing and watched it float silently into the darkness and disappear. It hadn't taken him long to do a preliminary inspection and work up a rough estimate. The house had been built to last, but had been neglected for several years. From what he could see on the surface alone, the repairs were going to be extensive, and there was no telling what he'd find once he started opening things up. With a crew of three men and himself, Gabe expected to be working here several weeks to bring the house to code and make it salable.

He glanced back at the front door. What the hell were they doing in there?

Soft, yellow light spilled from the living room window, and he edged his way across the porch. Just a peek, he told himself, to make sure Cara was handling the situation all right.

He tossed the cigar into the paper cup he'd brought out on the porch with him, heard the sizzle of the burning tip as it hit the remnants of his coffee.

Backing against the wall by the front door, he casually turned his head—

When the front door opened he jumped, then straightened quickly. One brow arched, Cara stood in the doorway, staring at him through the screen door. The woman, Melanie, stood beside her.

He leaned casually against the wall, crossing his arms over his chest as he glanced over at them with what he hoped was a bored expression.

"Melanie and Kevin will be spending the night here." The screen door screeched when Cara pushed it open and stepped out. "They're going to need some heat."

And? Gabe looked at his sister, waited for the tiniest morsel of information about Melanie and her son. Based on the expression on Cara's face, he obviously wasn't going to even get a tidbit.

He sighed, reached for the flashlight he'd set on the porch steps. "The pilot was shut off on the basement furnace. I'll go fire it up."

"That's not necessary." Melanie followed Cara out onto the porch. "We'll be fine. I have a blanket in my car."

Gabe's hand tightened around the flashlight. Had she and her son been sleeping in her car? And if so, why? Dammit, why wouldn't anyone tell him anything?

"It's no trouble," he said more tightly than he'd intended.

Cara placed her hand on Melanie's arm. "You'll be fine with Gabe," she said quietly. "I'd stay, but I have to be at the airport in an hour to pick up my husband, Ian, from a ten o'clock flight due in from New Jersey. We'll be coming back over here tomorrow morning after the board meeting. I'd like you to meet him."

Melanie shook her head. "I'll be leaving early."

Cara sighed. "You have my card. Call me anytime.

And my offer still stands. You and Kevin can stay here as long as you need to."

Melanie smiled weakly. "Thank you, but my friend is expecting us tomorrow. We'll be fine there."

Cara squeezed the woman's arm. "You promise to call and let me know you're both all right?"

"I will," Melanie said softly. "You've been so kind. Thank you again."

Cara hesitated, then slipped an arm around Melanie's slender shoulders and hugged her. The woman's eyes widened in surprise, then closed tightly as she hugged her back.

Gabe shifted uncomfortably, praying that neither woman would start with the waterworks. Damn, but he hated that. He'd rather walk barefoot through broken glass than deal with crying women.

He let out the breath he'd been holding when Cara and Melanie parted with dry eyes. Cara turned to him. "You have that report for me?"

"It's on your front seat." He gestured toward her silver van. "Do you want me to wait until after the board meeting, or get started right away?"

"Right away." She glanced up at the old house. "The meeting is just a formality. We have to do whatever needs to be done for resale."

He nodded, and she leaned toward him and gave him a hug. "Go easy with her," Cara whispered, and brushed his cheek with her lips. "And stop frowning."

What did his sister think he was going to do? he thought in annoyance as he watched her walk to her van. Lock the woman in the basement? Yell at her?

And just because he wasn't walking around with a

stupid grin on his face didn't mean he was frowning, either.

Waving, Cara pulled away with a crunch of tires on the gravel. He watched until the van's taillights disappeared and then he turned to Melanie, waited for her to speak. Folding her arms tightly in front of her, her gaze dropped to the worn wooden planks under her boots.

"Your sister is a wonderful person," she said quietly.

"She's a little bossy, but my brothers and I like her well enough."

Her gaze lifted to his. "Thank you for calling her."

Who are you, dammit? What kind of trouble are you in? All this politeness was killing him.

He nodded, but said nothing. The cold night air closed around them. Close by, in a grove of maples, a mockingbird began to sing.

Furrowing her brow, she took a step closer to him, her gaze leveled at his face. "Your cheek," she said, her eyes narrowed with concern. "I'm so sorry."

He touched the ragged scratch under his left eye. It stung a little, but wasn't all that deep. "You didn't do that. I caught the edge of a screen upstairs when I was climbing into the window."

She shook her head, frowned. "You wouldn't have had to climb in a window if I hadn't locked the doors. I—I'm sorry for the trouble I've caused you."

I don't want an apology. Just tell me why you're hiding in an empty house. What it is, or who, that you're afraid of.

He shrugged. "No trouble. It's just a scratch. Trust me, I've had worse."

"I…I didn't know if—" she paused, and her voice dropped to a whisper "—if I could trust you."

She still didn't trust him, he thought with more than a touch of annoyance. He felt the tension radiate from her, and could all but see the wall she'd erected around herself.

Why, dammit, why?

Oh, hell. What did it matter to him? They'd crossed paths, but she'd be gone in the morning, she and her son. Whatever her problem was, it was no concern of his. She didn't want his help, so why should he give it more than a passing thought? After tonight, he'd never see her again.

But did she have money? Gas in her car?

Hell.

Forget about it, Sinclair. Not your problem.

With her dark clothes and hair, she nearly blended in with the night. He watched her shiver, saw her breaths come out in little puffs of white and realized she was cold.

"I'll fire up the furnace now." He kept his voice even, controlled. "The house should warm up quickly. Is there anything else you need?"

As he'd known she would, she shook her head, but then surprised him by extending her hand. "Thank you for everything."

He hesitated, then took her hand.

And wished he hadn't.

Her hand was smooth against his, her fingers long and slender. Soft. In spite of the cold, her skin was warm, and the heat radiated up his arm, spread through his chest, then his body. She looked up at him, a mixture of confusion and amazement, then pulled her hand away and once again folded her arms tightly to her.

"I've got to go check on Kevin," she said, her voice a bit breathless. "Thank you again."

She turned and hurried back into the house. His eyes narrowed, then his fingers tightened around the flashlight in his hand until he heard the crack of plastic. He stood there for a long moment, waited until the overwhelming urge to follow her subsided.

Dammit, dammit, dammit.

He didn't even know her last name.

Cold fingers of pale dawn reached through the towering oak tree beside Mildred Witherspoon's weather-beaten detached garage. Frost covered the ankle-deep, weed-infested back lawn, sparkling like a crystal blanket in the early-morning light. Behind the garage, row after neat row of ceiling-high corn stretched acre after acre to a neighboring farm, where the steep black roof of a red barn peeked out from the tips of the silky stalks. Somewhere in the distance, Melanie heard the mournful moo of a cow.

Bucolic was the word that came to her mind as she stood at the back door and scanned the land. Like something she'd seen on a postcard or coffee table book of Midwest farms. She was a city girl, born and raised in Los Angeles, and what little traveling she had done, had never been to rural America. Phillip had always insisted on the exotic, the most elegant: Monte Carlo, New York, London, Washington D.C. Five-star hotels and expensive restaurants. Cows and cornstalks had not fit into her husband's fast-paced, sophisticated life-style.

And after that first, exciting year of their marriage,

Melanie thought wistfully, she hadn't fit very well, either.

She stepped out onto the back porch, sucked in a lungful of cold, crisp air, felt the rush of blood through her veins as her heart pounded awake. Shivering under the blue sweater she wore, she hurried down the porch steps and across a path of broken concrete that led to the garage, heard the crunch of early fall leaves under her boots. How she wished that she could linger, soak up every sight and sound of this peaceful place before she moved on.

But there was no time. She wanted to make Boston before dark, was certain that she would finally feel safe there with Raina. Raina was the only person Melanie could trust, the only real friend she'd ever had. They'd been best friends in high school, and after Melanie's father had died, and her mother remarried, Melanie had been at Raina's house more than she'd been at her own.

But so much had changed since then. They'd both gone in different directions after high school. Raina had gone to Greece and modeled for a short time before marrying, then she'd divorced and started working as a clothing designer for a company in Italy. Melanie had married Phillip and had a baby. Raina had never even seen Kevin.

Melanie smiled as she thought of her son. She'd left him bundled up and sleeping on the sofa in the living room. He hadn't even stirred when she'd carried him down from one of the upstairs bedrooms where they'd slept last night. Well, where he'd slept, anyway. Even though she'd locked all the doors and windows, checked them twice, she'd still tossed and turned most of the night, listening to every creak and groan of the drafty old house.

Listening for doors opening…footsteps.

The icy chill slithering up her spine had nothing to do with the cold, she knew.

Rubbing her arms, she pulled her car keys out of her front jeans' pocket and opened the small entry door on the side of the garage. The overhead door was closed, and it was dark and cold inside. She scanned the shadows, holding her breath, then quickly releasing it when she was satisfied no one was hiding there.

When will I have to stop looking over my shoulder? she wondered.

Maybe never, she thought with a weary sigh. Or at least not until Louise was dead, and even though the woman was seventy-four, she was in the best of health. Physically, at least. Melanie knew that her mother-in-law would never stop looking for her and Kevin. She had the tenacity of a bulldog and, when threatened, the same vicious bite.

She was also crazy, a slow deterioration of her mind since the loss of her husband to cancer three years earlier, then her only son two years later. But crazy people with as much money and connections as Louise Van Camp had were usually considered eccentric. Everyone looked the other way, especially when it benefited their pocketbooks.

Shivering again, Melanie slid into the front seat of her car. It was a sturdy little Honda Accord, silver-blue, and had run like a dream across the country. She'd bought it from a private party in the classifieds, and she'd paid cash. She had the pink slip, but she hadn't registered it yet. Which meant the only name on the car was still the previous owner. There would be no DMV record until she did register the car—which she had no intention of doing for a long time. And when she did, it wouldn't be under the name of Melissa Van Camp.

The only problem with the car had been that it wasn't big enough to bring much more than the barest essentials. She'd left most of hers and Kevin's belongings at Louise's estate in Beverly Hills. But what had it mattered? Most of those things had been given to her by Louise or Phillip and meant nothing to her. They would start fresh in Boston, where Raina was temporarily working for an exclusive shop that specialized in custom evening wear. In three months, Raina would go back to Italy, and she'd been pleading with Melanie for her and Kevin to go with her.

A new beginning, Melanie thought. It frightened her, but she could do it. For Kevin, she could do anything.

The only thing that mattered, the only thing important to her, was her son. Kevin was her love, her life, and no one, *no one,* was going to take him away from her.

Her teeth were chattering as she slid the key into the ignition and turned it to start the engine.

It made a low, grinding sound, then nothing.

Her heart pounding, she turned the key again, heard nothing but the sound of a click.

"No!" she said aloud, pumping the gas pedal. "No, no, *no!*"

Nothing.

On a half-sob, she laid her head down on the steering wheel and gulped in deep breaths of cold air. She was torn between laughing hysterically and crying, then settled for anger. Jumping out of the car, she balled her hands into fists and slammed them down on the roof.

"You miserable son of a bitch!"

The expletive bounced off the garage walls like a pinball, then shot out the open side door.

Gabe had parked his truck behind the garage and was climbing out of the cab, a cup of coffee in his hand, when Melanie's castigation had his head turning. *What in the world…?*

Another salvo of insults broke the still of the morning, and he headed for the garage.

"You can't do this to me." He heard her voice rise with fury. "You *can't.* Not now. I won't let you."

Was she with someone? he wondered. Or arguing with someone on a cell phone? He walked to the open door, saw her fingers rake through that glorious, thick sable hair of hers while she paced beside a blue compact. California license plates, he noted.

"I need you," she said, her voice rough with desperation. "Please, I need you."

His fingers tightened on the mug in his hand. So there *was* a man involved in whatever trouble she was in, he thought, and wondered what kind of man would abandon a woman and child. Not a man, he decided. A snake, maybe, or something lower, something that lived under a rock and left a trail of slime. Anger narrowed his eyes and stiffened his jaw. He didn't know the guy, but he'd like five minutes alone with the jerk.

It twisted his gut to hear this woman plead, but it also surprised him. Of all the things he'd seen in Melanie last night, it certainly hadn't been defeat or acquiescence. Even when he'd had her cornered, she'd come out swinging. She hadn't begged or pleaded. She'd stood up to him.

Damn if he hadn't admired that.

"Now you listen to me," she said, the anger back in her voice. "You will start, and you will run smooth as a top. Do you hear me?"

Her hands settled on her narrow hips as she faced the Honda and Gabe realized that she was talking to the *car,* not a man.

I'll be damned, he thought, and struggled to keep his lips from twitching.

"The next farm over hears you," he said, taking a sip of his coffee as he leaned against the doorjamb. "How 'bout I go get some boxing gloves and you two duke it out?"

On a gasp, she whirled, eyes wide and faced him. Her hand flew to her chest, and the breath she'd sucked in came shuddering out. "You scared me," she whispered hoarsely.

"Sorry." He grinned at her. "I wasn't sure if I was going to have to pull you off someone or referee."

Even in the dim light of the garage, Gabe could see the color rise on Melanie's high cheeks. Her skin was porcelain smooth against her dark hair, her gray eyes tinged with blue, the same smoky blue as the sweater she wore. When his gaze drifted to her mouth, he realized that was dangerous territory and he quickly looked away.

"What seems to be the problem?" He pushed away from the doorjamb.

"It...it won't start."

"Pop the hood." He stepped toward the front of the car, waited while she reached inside and pulled the hood release. "Now try to start it again."

A small grind, then nothing.

She moved beside him, hands shoved into the back pockets of her jeans, obviously unaware that the stance emphasized the rise of full breasts under her sweater and also clearly revealed the fact that she was cold.

He ignored the quick twist in his gut and focused on the engine, checking the battery and cables. ''Battery,'' he said after a moment. ''I could jump it, but this battery is toast, and it wouldn't hold.''

She'd moved beside him to watch what he'd been doing, and his words made her eyes close on a heavy sigh. Her shoulders sagged as if she carried the weight of the world there. The top of her head lined up with his chin and he looked down at her, caught the faint scent of flowers again, subtle, but sweet. Unwillingly he drew the scent in, held it.

When she opened her eyes again, she turned and looked up at him. Her composure was back, the anger that had sparked her eyes when she'd been yelling was gone now, in its place, a weary acceptance. The faint smudge of circles under her eyes told him she hadn't slept well. Strangely, and much to his annoyance, he hadn't slept well, either.

He'd told himself last night, then all the way over here that he didn't give a damn if she was still at the house when he got here this morning. He had work to do, and a woman and kid would just be in the way. He liked working alone, which was why he'd chosen renovating homes for Sinclair Construction instead of working in the office, which was Callan's department, or new construction, which Lucian seemed to enjoy.

On a bigger job, like the Witherspoon house, Gabe would work often with a small crew, but usually he worked by himself. Came and went as he pleased, worked at his own pace, and rarely had to watch over anyone or ride herd. He'd done enough of that trying to keep the family together after his parents had died, and with a fifteen-year-old stubborn, independent sister to raise, he'd more than had his hands full.

He liked being alone now. He liked the quiet, the calm. No responsibilities but his own.

"Thank you," Melanie said, pulling Gabe from his wandering mind. "I'll handle it from here."

"I can call the repair shop in town," he offered. "Have them deliver a battery."

Shaking her head, she forced a smile, and much to Gabe's relief, folded her arms over her breasts. "Thanks, but I'd rather take care of this myself."

She wanted to take care of everything herself, Gabe thought with annoyance. And while that was an admirable trait, it could also be carried just a little too far.

He closed the hood, offered her the cup of coffee in his hands. When she opened her mouth to say no, he shoved it at her. "You're cold," he said firmly. "This is hot. Drink it."

She hesitated, then wrapped her hands around the mug and brought it to her mouth. Gabe felt an unwilling tug of desire when her lips touched the brim, and when she licked those lips a moment later and smiled at him, the tug turned sharp.

And that irritated him more than Melanie's stubborn independence.

"Is it a husband?" he asked tightly, watched her smile fade.

"Excuse me?"

"Are you running away from a husband?" He had to know, dammit. He *had* to know.

She handed the cup back to him. "Thank you for your help, Mr. Sinclair. I know you have work to do, so if you'll excuse me, I need to get back to my son."

"Look, Melanie—" He started to reach for her, but when she stiffened, he drew his hand back. "Dammit, I don't even know your last name."

She turned, walked to the door, then paused before she turned back. "Hart," she said quietly. "My name is Melanie Hart."

She was gone then, though he heard the crunch of her boots on the path leading to the house, then the quiet squeak of the back screen door.

He looked at the coffee cup in his hand, resisted the urge to throw it against something.

She didn't want his help. Fine. Just fine. Let her figure it out herself.

Dammit.

He tossed back a gulp of coffee, then stared at the spot where her lips had touched.

Dammit, dammit.

Still muttering curses, he walked back to his truck and drove away.

From inside the house, Melanie heard the roar of Gabe's truck engine, then the spin of wheels as he drove off. She hadn't wanted to be rude, it wasn't in her nature at all. If anything, she'd been overly polite her entire life, which had partly created the horrible mess she was in now. She'd said yes too many times, let too many people tell her what to do and how to do it. She knew she was overcompensating by refusing to accept any help now, but she didn't know what else to do. She wasn't certain she had enough money left for a battery, and she certainly couldn't expect strangers to loan her money, though that was exactly what Gabe's sister had offered to do last night.

It was so damn humiliating. So damn frustrating.

She'd told Cara only the barest facts about her situation last night, that she'd left a difficult situation with a dominating mother-in-law behind her in California, that she was trying to make a new life for herself and Kevin as far away from there as she could get. That she wanted, *needed,* to make it on her own, without any help.

But she hadn't told Cara what extremes Louise had gone to, or would go to. She hadn't told her about Vincent Drake, her mother-in-law's so-called business manager who was no more than a hired thug, a monster that Louise had employed to see that the recalcitrant daughter-in-law and her grandson came back home.

Melanie couldn't tell Cara any of that, there was no reason to involve any more innocent people. Melanie had already seen what happened to anyone who tried to help her. One friend had already suffered a broken arm and black eye for helping her, another had been threatened. And the fire.

She shuddered thinking what might have happened if the fire department hadn't arrived at her apartment so quickly after Vincent had lit that match to her drapes. How many people might have lost their homes and belongings, maybe even their lives? She couldn't let anyone else be hurt because of her.

She just needed to get to Raina's. Louise didn't know about her best friend. With the new ID and a fake social security number Melanie had purchased from the back room of a seedy bar in Los Angeles, she and Kevin would start a new life. She was Melanie Hart now. She never wanted to be Melissa Van Camp again. That woman no longer existed.

But if she was ever going to get to Boston, she had to get her car fixed first. And she intended to do that, only she was suddenly so tired, she couldn't think straight.

She moved into the living room and sat down beside her still sleeping son. She watched him, let her gaze wander over his dimpled cheeks and short freckled nose, felt the peace come over her. She laid her head back and closed her eyes.

She just needed a few minutes of rest, she thought. Then her mind would be clear. She'd gotten Kevin and herself this far.

She had no intention of giving up now.

Chapter 3

"You've been a bad girl, Melanie," Vincent whispered. "A bad, bad girl."

Like a snake, his voice slithered up from the darkness. She couldn't see him, but she felt him, felt the icy-cold hiss of his breath on her neck.

Run! her mind screamed, but the dirt under her feet turned to mud and sucked at her legs, drawing her down into the thick muck. Her arms hung like lead at her sides, useless, helpless.

Kevin ran out of the thick forest toward her, smiling, his arms raised. She opened her mouth to scream, tell him to run away, but no sound came.

"You know what happens to bad girls?" Vincent warned, his disembodied voice low and sinister. "Shall I show you?"

Powerless to stop him, she heard her own whimper. Like a spider's legs, his fingers brushed over her cheek, then wrapped around her neck.

Still smiling, Kevin jumped into her arms, but she couldn't catch him, couldn't hold him…

Melanie jerked awake, her heart pounding furiously. Kevin lay in her arms, giggling as he tickled her cheek with the tip of his finger.

A dream, only a dream, she told herself, even though it had seemed so real. The same dream she'd had so many nights. The same nightmare. She wrapped her arms tightly around her son, drawing deep, calming breaths as she drew him close. He tolerated the hug for all of five seconds before protesting and pushing himself away.

At the sudden bang at the back door, she jumped, once again grabbed Kevin and dragged him into her arms.

"Hey, get the door for me, will you?" Melanie heard Gabe yell.

With Kevin following closely behind in his flannel Batman pajamas, Melanie glanced at her wristwatch as she hurried to the back door. Nine o'clock! She'd been asleep over an hour, she realized, and groaned aloud at the loss of precious time.

She flipped the latch up, then opened the door. Gabe stood on the other side of the screen door, one brown paper grocery bag in each arm and two plastic bags hanging from each hand.

"Thanks." He smiled at her, then glanced down at Kevin. "Mornin', Batman."

Kevin's dimples flashed, and he grabbed hold of the hem of her sweater, hugging close.

"Do you mind?" Gabe gestured toward the screen door and Melanie pushed it open wide, then moved out of the way.

He stepped around them and strode into the

kitchen, bringing the clean smell of country air with him. With a *thud,* he dumped the groceries onto the kitchen table that sat in the middle of the large, airy room. One bag turned over, and three cans of peas rolled across the bleached pine tabletop. Before they could crash to the hardwood floor, Gabe snatched them up, sang *da dada da, da dada da,* while juggling them like a circus act, then tossed them back into the bag one at a time. Grinning, he spread his hands wide.

Well, *his* mood certainly had changed.

His mouth open, Kevin stared, then laughed. Even Melanie couldn't help the smile pulling at the corners of her mouth.

"And for my next trick—" Gabe pulled a carton of eggs out of a bag "—you and I are going to make these eggs disappear."

"We are?" Kevin's blue eyes were wide with wonder.

Gabe nodded. "Right after your mommy cooks them up into great big ham and cheese omelettes."

Kevin giggled, and Gabe swept his gaze to Melanie. "Please tell me you know how to cook."

There was a lightness to his tone, but the intense, sharp look in his forest-green eyes made her breath catch. He was offering his help, but at the same time, making it clear he wasn't going to push. She already understood this man well enough to know that was not an easy thing for him. Gabriel Sinclair was a man who wanted to be in charge, who *needed* to be in charge.

Which was exactly the last thing she wanted, and the last thing she needed.

She sighed. But she and Kevin needed to eat, and she could rationalize that cooking a meal for Gabe was paying her way for food for her son and herself. Besides, she certainly wasn't going anywhere until the battery was replaced on her car. A meal would fortify her, get her brain working again so she could deal with her most current crisis.

She met his gaze, lifted one corner of her mouth. "You sure you want ham in that omelette?" she asked sweetly. "It seems to me you've got plenty of that already."

He lifted one brow, and she saw the glint of amusement in his eyes. "Lots of ham, darlin', and extra cheese. A growing boy needs protein. Isn't that right, Kevin?"

One long cowlick, dead center in the middle of Kevin's sandy blond head, wiggled as he nodded enthusiastically, though Melanie knew her son didn't have a clue what protein was.

When Gabe started to unload the food, Melanie reached out and took the package of cheese from his hand, accidentally brushing her fingertips with his.

There it was again, she thought with a catch of her breath. That same jolt of heat she'd felt when they'd shook hands last night. She thought that maybe she'd been overwrought and had simply overreacted to his touch, or that she'd even imagined it.

But she hadn't imagined it. *It,* whatever *it* was, was definitely there. It zapped her fingertips, then shot straight down to her toes like electricity through a wire.

She tugged the package of already shredded cheese from his hand. "I know you have work to do here. I'll put these things away, then see if I can find my way around this kitchen."

He stared at her for what seemed like a lifetime,

though it probably wasn't more than three or four seconds. The playfulness she'd seen in his eyes only moments ago was gone now. In its place was something dark and intense.

Despite the heavy thud of her heart in her chest, she forced a smile. "It shouldn't be too long. I'll call you when it's ready."

At last, with a nod, he turned and headed for the door leading to the living room. She released the breath she'd been holding.

"Gabe."

He stopped at her quiet call, glanced over his shoulder.

"You asked me earlier and I didn't answer you then. I don't have a husband."

She waited, frozen in place under his penetrating gaze.

"Good," he said simply, then turned and was gone.

Melanie stared at the empty doorway, waiting for the floor under her feet to gain substance again. She could still feel the tingle from his touch shimmering over her skin.

"Mommy, did you see what that man did? Did you see?" Kevin tugged on her sweater. "That was so neat!"

"Yes, sweetie, I saw." She glanced down at her son, ran a hand over his rumpled hair. "Very neat."

"I'm a growing boy," Kevin said firmly. "Can I have lots of ham and cheese in my omelette, too? Just like him?"

Melanie wasn't sure she liked the "just like him" part of her son's request, but it had been a long time since she'd seen him excited about anything, including food. The first time since Phillip had died and Louise had moved into their lives that she'd seen her son's big blue eyes sparkle.

"Sure you can." Smiling, Melanie took Kevin's chin in her hand and tipped his face up as she bent down to kiss his nose. "One double cheese and ham omelette coming right up."

The sound of a door opening and closing upstairs caught Melanie's attention. *Two* omelettes coming up, she corrected herself, then forced herself to concentrate on the task at hand, not the lingering feel of Gabe Sinclair's fingers against her own.

Gabe lay on his back under the upstairs bathroom sink, a wrench in one hand and a rag in the other. He'd been trying to loosen the rusted pipe for the past fifteen minutes, with no success. Gritting his teeth, he pulled tightly on the wrench, but the stubborn pipe refused to budge. *Dammit.*

Must be female, he thought irritably, grunting as he bore down, but the wrench twisted off and struck him square on the jaw.

Son of a bitch! His vision exploded with stars, and his jaw throbbed from the blow. Dragging himself out from under the sink, he sat, head down between his knees and swore hotly.

Definitely female, Gabe decided.

With a heavy sigh, he raked a hand through his hair. The most amazing smells were wafting up from downstairs. He sucked the delicious aromas into his lungs and held them there. His stomach began to rumble like a freight train.

Thank God she hadn't turned tail and run when he'd asked her to cook. He'd certainly expected her to, had been surprised when she'd agreed. But he'd been even more surprised when she'd actually teased him about the ham. There was a playful side to Melanie Hart, he realized, though she was doing her best to keep it hidden.

Along with the rest of her secrets.

He hadn't told her that he'd already bought a battery for her car, as well, and that he intended to install it for her, with or without her approval. He figured he'd lay that one on her after breakfast. One tiny step at a time with this woman.

I don't have a husband.

Her quiet words had been running through his mind like one of those little hamsters on a wheel. And running along right beside her declaration was the burning question: What was her problem?

He'd called Cara late last night, hoping to get some answers, but she'd been tight-lipped. She told him that if Melanie wanted him to know something, then she'd tell him herself.

Yeah. Right. That would happen right about the same time that the IRS told him it was no longer necessary for him to pay taxes. Just because he was such a nice guy.

It had been a natural assumption that Melanie was hiding out from an abusive husband, Gabe thought. But unless she was lying—and he was as certain as he could be she wasn't—then the husband theory was wrong.

So was she in trouble with the law?

It was strictly a gut feeling, but he didn't think so, even though she'd been so panicked last night when she thought he was calling the police. He'd seen how gentle she was with her son, how tender. Gabe touched the scratch on his cheek, remembered her concern when she'd seen the blood on his face and she'd thought she'd hurt him. Even her attempt to bean him with that statue had been halfhearted. He couldn't believe for a second that this woman was a criminal.

But if it wasn't a husband, and it wasn't the police, then what was it?

None of his business, that's what it was. He rubbed his sore jaw. She'd be on the road as soon as he installed her battery, which would be right after breakfast. So what was the point in all this speculation? It was doing him no good to think beyond the present moment with Melanie. No damn good at all.

He stared at his hand, remembered the touch of her fingertips on his. The contact had been brief, a mere brush of skin, but damn if something hadn't passed between them, something downright...unnerving.

The same as last night, when he'd shaken her hand.

There was lust, of course. He recognized that clearly enough. He'd been down that road more than a few times with a woman. But lust had never thrown him off balance like this before. Had never hit him in the solar plexus like a two-by-four.

Weird, that's what it was.

"Are you all right?"

He glanced up at the sound of Melanie's voice. She stood in the doorway, hands linked behind her.

"I thought I heard you bellow," she said as her gaze took in the wrench in his hand.

"I'm fighting about thirty years of rust," he said with a shrug.

"Looks like you lost." She nodded toward his jaw.

"Just the battle, not the war." Rubbing his chin,

he rose, tossed the wrench back into his toolbox. "I'll be back, packing a bigger wrench."

Smiling softly, she glanced around the spacious bathroom, her gaze pausing at the porcelain claw foot bathtub that sat in the middle of the white tile floor, then moving on to linger and obviously admire an antique, cherry wood armoire with carved panels. A matching dressing table with a beveled mirror sat on the wall opposite the armoire. Gabe watched Melanie's soft gray eyes widen at the assortment of crystal perfume bottles and elegant silver brushes and combs that lay on top of the dresser.

An image of Melanie sitting at the dressing table popped into Gabe's head. She wore white silk and lace; her dark hair was swept up, exposing her long, slender neck. She touched the tip of perfumed crystal just below the delicate curve of her ear. Damn if he couldn't even smell the sweet scent that drifted from her.

He blinked, then snapped his thoughts back to the present. Weird.

"Funny." Gabe stared at the dressing table. "I wouldn't have thought old lady Witherspoon was a silver brush, crystal perfume bottle kind of woman."

"She was a nice lady," Melanie said thoughtfully.

Nice lady? Gabe had heard Miss Witherspoon called a lot of things, but never nice. Then it dawned on him exactly what Melanie had just said. "You *did* know her?"

"I knew her," she said quietly, then pulled her gaze from the dresser. "Breakfast is ready."

He watched her turn and go back downstairs. He'd assumed that she'd been lying when she'd said that she knew the elderly woman. But how did Melanie know Mildred Witherspoon? he wondered. As far as he knew, Mildred had never left Bloomfield County. Other than church, town meetings and an occasional doctor appointment, it was a well-known fact that the woman rarely went out. For the past few years, she'd even had her groceries delivered directly to her house.

Gabe stared at the empty doorway where Melanie had been standing. And if he was certain of anything, it was that Melanie Hart had never been to Bloomfield County before.

Don't ask, Sinclair. If she wants you to know, she'll tell you.

With a sigh, Gabe made his way downstairs and found her in the kitchen, by the sink, her arms folded as she stared down at her son. Kevin had changed into a white T-shirt with a picture of Batman on the front, blue jeans and tennis shoes. His little hands were shoved deeply into the front pockets of his jeans.

"I just washed my hands," Kevin said firmly.

Melanie frowned. "You washed them last night. You have to wash them again, before you eat."

Ah, the age-old argument. Gabe suppressed a smile as he watched mother and son. Stubborn appeared to be a strong gene in Melanie and her son, he thought, recognizing the determined tilt of Kevin's chin.

"Sure smells good." Gabe strolled casually into the room, rolling up the sleeves of his blue denim shirt. Kevin and Melanie stepped out of his way when he moved to the sink. "I'm so hungry, I could eat a whole cow."

Kevin stared up at him, eyes wide. "We're not having cow. We're having omelettes. Remember?"

"Well, I could eat a whole omelette then." Gabe turned on the sink faucet, made a note that the washers needed replacing as he reached for a new bar of white soap on the ledge. "Soon as I wash my hands."

Kevin pressed his lips tightly together. Even at four, he obviously recognized a con job. "*My* hands aren't dirty. I already washed them."

"Kevin—" Melanie warned.

"So did I." Gabe worked up a foamy froth of suds. "But Batman says he always washes his hands right exactly the minute before he eats."

Kevin stared at him with suspicion in his big blue eyes. "Batman says that?"

"Yep."

"Why?"

Gabe glanced at Melanie, who was watching the two of them with interest and amusement. "Well, it's kind of a secret—" Gabe lowered his voice, leaned closer to Kevin "—but the reason is that when he eats with clean hands, it makes him strong, and that's how he catches all the bad guys."

The freckles on Kevin's nose wrinkled as he scrunched up his face in deep thought. He looked at his mother, back at Gabe, then pulled his hands out of his pockets and stuck them under the running water. Gabe handed him the soap, and Kevin turned the big white bar over and over in his little hands, attempting to work up the same frothy lather that Gabe had.

Pleased with his success, Gabe looked over at Melanie, expecting her expression to be approval and admiration for his cunning. But her expression was closer to worry. An uneasiness that narrowed her eyes and pressed her lips into a thin line.

What the hell had he said?

"I'll put the food on the table while you two finish

up,'' she said without meeting his curious gaze, then turned away and moved toward the stove, a white-enameled gas range that had to be at least fifty years old. The refrigerator also appeared to be as ancient, he noticed. Not a microwave or blender in sight. It appeared that Mildred Witherspoon did not subscribe to modern conveniences.

Kevin, meanwhile, had decided he didn't just want his hands clean, he wanted them extra-extra squeaky clean. Delighted with the translucent bubbles billowing from his soapy hands, he continued to scrub and wash.

''I think we've got it now, partner.'' Gabe rinsed the child's hands, then dried them off. ''We've still got to make those omelettes disappear, remember?''

Kevin ran to the table and climbed up on a ladder-back wooden chair. Gabe turned to help Melanie, who was busy at the stove, but she waved him to sit, so he did. Two seconds later, she set a heaping plate of sliced potatoes with onions and peppers and a big fluffy omelette in front of him and told him to eat. He took a bite of the eggs and closed his eyes on a sigh. Scooping up a biteful of potatoes, he actually moaned.

Lord, but he'd died and gone to heaven.

''Damn, woman,'' he said around another bite, ''if you cook this good, I'm going to have to marry you right now.''

Gabe watched as Kevin's eyes opened wide, then noticed Melanie had sternly arched one eyebrow.

''Hey,'' he said awkwardly, ''I was just—''

''He said damn,'' Kevin announced.

Had he? Oops.

"You're not supposed to say damn," Kevin admonished.

"Kevin," Melanie said firmly as she sat at the table with a plate of food for Kevin and herself. "You don't tell adults what they can or can't say. And you most certainly don't repeat bad words."

"You mean like those other words Gabe said earlier when he was upstairs?" Kevin asked.

"Especially those," Melanie said.

Remembering a few of those words, Gabe ducked his head sheepishly. He hadn't considered that anyone else had heard, and hell—heck—he wasn't used to being around kids.

"Sorry," he muttered.

"It's okay." Kevin took a bite of potatoes. "Sometimes my mommy says bad words, too. Especially when she got into that big fight with Grandma Louise before we had to move away. She said a bunch of bad words then, but she didn't think I heard."

"Kevin Andrew!" Melanie narrowed a sharp look at her son. "That's enough."

Her tone brooked no argument, and Kevin looked down at his plate. Color had risen on Melanie's cheeks, but it was apparent to Gabe that her concern had much less to do with her use of bad words than it did with Kevin's mention of her argument with his grandma. An argument that it seemed had precipitated Melanie and her son's flight.

But it was hardly logical that Melanie would pack her belongings in a car and take off with her son because she and her mother—or mother-in-law—disagreed about something, Gabe thought. Families fought all the time. Lord knew his certainly did. Well, except for Cara. Who could argue with Cara? She had a way of either smiling that cut straight into your heart, or giving you "the look" that cut straight across the knees. But he and his brothers preferred to settle their disputes with a lot of yelling and occasionally a fist flew. But they never held grudges. Well, maybe Lucian did, but only for a few days at the most.

Not that Gabe knew what Melanie and Kevin's grandma had argued about, but running away never seemed to solve anything. And somehow, Melanie just didn't strike Gabe as the type to run. She seemed much too strong, too stubborn to let anyone intimidate her.

He knew he hadn't.

And he'd certainly tried.

He watched her now, saw her gaze settle intently on the cell phone he'd slipped into the pocket of his shirt. With no working phone here at the house, and stranded the way she was, it wasn't difficult for him to figure out that she wanted to make a call but couldn't bring herself to ask.

He sighed silently, pulled the phone out of his pocket and set it on the table between them. "Help yourself."

Surprised, her eyes snapped up to meet his. She hesitated, then nodded stiffly. "Thank you."

It was all he could do not to put his hands on her shoulders and try to shake a little sense into her, tell her that she could trust him, and that running wouldn't solve anything.

But he also realized that he wanted to put his hands on her for other reasons. Reasons that had nothing to do with her secrets, and everything to do with that incredible mouth of hers and how much he wanted to taste those lips.

Gabe knew he was going to have more than one sleepless night thinking about those lips after she left, and the realization aggravated the hell out of him.

He decided he wanted her gone. The sooner the better. He didn't need the distraction, and he sure as hell didn't need the complication. He wanted his life to be simple and easy, and this woman was anything but.

"The parts store will be delivering a battery for your car here later on this morning," he said firmly. "I'll put it in for you when it gets here."

She protested, of course, and he ignored her, felt a certain amount of smugness when she appeared as frustrated as he was. He finished his meal, then muttered a quick thanks and headed back to the upstairs bathroom.

He had the rusted pipe off in less than a minute, but he bloodied four of his knuckles in the process. And somehow managed to bite back every obscene word that danced on the tip of his tongue.

Her sweater sleeves pushed to her elbows, her hands plunged in hot, sudsy dishwater, Melanie scrubbed at the heavy cast-iron frying pan, thankful that she had a task to occupy not only her hands, but her mind, as well.

Anything to keep her thoughts off Gabe Sinclair.

The man simply filled a room. Not just because he was tall and broad, but because he had a presence, a larger-than-life demeanor that overwhelmed her. All he had to do was level that dark gaze of his at her and she felt...consumed.

She couldn't find her balance when he was around, couldn't think straight. And she needed to think straight. She couldn't afford not to. For her own sake, and especially for Kevin's.

Behind her, sitting on his knees in a chair at the kitchen table, her son hummed the Barney theme song while he colored a picture in his travel game book. Silly songs and that big game book had been two things that made the trip cross-country bearable. Though if she never heard that Barney song again in her life, that would be just fine with her.

She rinsed the pan and drained the sink, then wiped her hands on a dish towel. Gabe's cell phone still lay on the table where he'd left it for her. She hadn't asked, but he'd known that she'd wanted to use it. She hated that she'd been so visible, that he knew what she was thinking, what she needed. What else did he see? she wondered, and the thought frightened her.

Almost as much as his insistence at buying and installing a battery for her car frustrated her.

She'd never met a man like him in her entire life, she thought with a sigh.

"Mommy's going to make a phone call," she said to Kevin, and he merely bobbed his head in response. Melanie picked up the phone, heard the clink of pipes overhead and glanced up at the ceiling before she moved into the laundry room connected to the kitchen, left the door ajar so she could keep an eye on her son.

She dialed, waited three rings.

"Hello."

Just the sound of her friend's voice brought tears to her eyes. "Rae, it's me."

"Melissa! Thank God, I've been so worried about you. Are you all right?"

"I'm fine," she said through the thickness in her throat. "But the battery in my car died, and it's being replaced today. I may not get there until tomorrow."

"Mel." Raina lowered her voice. "Oh, honey, I'm so sorry, but you can't come here. I think someone's watching my apartment."

Melanie went still, then felt her heart slam against her ribs. "What?"

"Three days ago I noticed a gray sedan parked a block away with a man inside. I didn't think too much about it at first, but I saw the car again yesterday, then again today, always parked in a different place, but close enough to see anyone coming and going from my complex. Always with someone sitting inside."

Oh, God, no. Melanie squeezed her eyes shut. How could Louise have found Raina? She had a different last name since she'd married briefly while living in Greece that one summer. She was Raina Sarbanes now, not Raina Williams. She'd been out of the country for seven years.

How? How could they have found her?

Vincent, she thought with a shiver. Vincent was everywhere, knew everything.

"Mel...are you there? Mel! Talk to me!"

"What?" Melanie pressed a hand to her temple, sucked in a breath. "Oh, Rae, God, I'm so sorry. I never thought they'd find out about you. Especially since we'd lost touch after all those years."

"Thanks to that jerk husband of yours," Raina said bitterly, then sighed. "Sorry, Mel."

Melanie thought of all the phone messages from Raina that Phillip had never given her, the letters he'd sent back. He'd wanted his wife all to himself, and she'd been too blind to see what he'd been doing. Until Kevin was born. Everything had changed after that. And then it was too late.

She glanced at her son, still working intently on his picture. He'd caught his lower lip between his teeth while he scribbled with a blue crayon. He looked just like Phillip, she thought. The sandy-blond hair, blue eyes, the angular shape of his jaw. One day her little boy would be a handsome, mature man who would have women falling at his feet, just like his daddy had.

No, *not* like his daddy, she thought resolutely. Kevin didn't have the selfish, cruel streak in him that Phillip had. When it came to personality, father and son were as opposite as night and day. Kevin was genuinely loving and sweet. Phillip's charm had been practiced and phony. Manipulative.

"Mel, for God's sake, stay with me here!"

Melanie snapped her thoughts back to the moment. She couldn't think about the past now. It would only weaken her, drag her down. She needed to be strong, to think.

"I'm here." Melanie tightened her hand on the phone.

"All right, now listen to me," Raina said firmly, and Melanie could almost see her friend pointing one long perfectly manicured fingernail at her. "I'll take care of this bozo, but just to be safe, you better not come to my place right now. Call me in a few days, and I'll have a new plan by then."

"No," Melanie said around the lump in her throat. "I can't allow you to get involved anymore. I told you what happened to Paul when he tried to help me. I won't take any more chances."

"Don't you talk like that, do you hear me? I won't just stand by and let these horrible—"

"I've got to go." Melanie blinked back the threatening tears. "I'll call you in a few days when I've figured something out."

"Please, Mel, don't hang up, please. Let me help."

"You can't," Melanie said quietly. *No one can.* "Kevin and I will be fine. Don't worry."

"I'm going to go to California and wring Louise's neck," Raina said furiously. "Then I'm going to pluck the old hen naked, stuff her and throw her in..."

Raina went on in gruesome detail and in spite of the situation, Melanie couldn't help but smile at Raina's tirade. She'd always had a temper, and obviously, still did.

"I love you, too," Melanie said, then flipped the phone off.

Closing her eyes, she slowly, carefully drew in a long breath, then released it. She would figure something out. In just a minute. Or two. As soon as her mind stopped spinning.

At the staccato sound of a car's horn, her eyes flew open. She felt a moment of dread, but realized that Vincent certainly wouldn't announce himself in such a conspicuous manner. Whoever it was, they belonged here. Unlike herself, she thought.

She drew in another breath, stepped out of the laundry room and closed the door behind her.

And never once realized that the laundry room vent over her head linked directly to the bathroom upstairs.

Chapter 4

When Gabe came down the stairs, Cara was standing in the entryway. She normally dressed casually, in jeans and sweaters or long skirts, but today she had on a teal business suit that made her green eyes sparkle, and he realized she'd come here straight from her board meeting with the foundation.

She had a coffeemaker in one hand and a box of doughnuts in the other.

"My kind of woman." Gabe grinned and reached for the doughnut box. "Too bad you're my sister."

She tightened her hold on the box. "I've said that countless times myself. Keep out of this box until the coffee's made."

His arms loaded with bags of groceries, Ian pushed the door open with his shoulder and stood beside his wife. At six-four, Ian stood a good eight inches taller than Cara. His hair was dark, hers blond. They looked good together, Gabe thought, though the first time he'd met Ian he'd wanted to punch the guy's lights out for sleeping with his baby sister. Never mind she'd been twenty-six at the time and living on her own—she was still his baby sister. As far as he was concerned, she would always be his baby sister.

"She slapped my hand all the way from Philly," Ian said sourly. "Wouldn't even let me have a nibble."

Cara looked at her husband. "We got the doughnuts in Bloomfield, not Philly."

He wiggled his eyebrows and grinned. "Who's talking about doughnuts?"

"Men." Cara rolled her eyes. "Food and sex. Is there nothing else?"

Ian and Gabe looked at each other blankly, then Gabe said, "The Cards are playing the Expos tonight. Reese has a pool going. You in?"

Ian nodded. "Ten bucks."

Shaking her head, Cara shoved the coffeepot at Gabe. "Make yourself useful. Where's Melanie and Kevin?"

"We're right here."

All three heads turned at the sound of Melanie's voice. She stood in the dining room, with Kevin in her arms.

"Hey, big guy." Cara smiled at Kevin. "I sure hope you like chocolate doughnuts with lots of colored sprinkles."

Kevin's eyes lit up.

"This is my husband, Ian." Cara slipped a hand through his arm. "Ian, this is Melanie and Kevin."

Melanie smiled stiffly.

She looked like she wanted to bolt, Gabe thought irritably. And since he'd overheard most of her phone call from the vent in the upstairs bathroom, he had a pretty good idea of where it was she was so damn anxious to get to.

She might not have a husband, but it certainly appeared that she had a boyfriend. One that she didn't want anyone to know about. Gabe had heard bits and pieces of her conversation, especially the "I love you" and "I never thought they would find out" parts.

A married man, he thought grimly. That would explain her need for secrecy.

And for the hundredth time that morning alone, he reminded himself that it was none of his damn business. The woman could do whatever she damn well pleased. It was no skin off his nose. None at all.

Gabe moved toward Melanie, but kept his eyes on Kevin. "We don't get doughnuts until the coffee is made. You wanna help?"

Kevin stuck his finger into his mouth, then his head bounced with a yes.

"Okay, partner." With his free arm, Gabe scooped Kevin out of Melanie's hold and carried him under his arm like a sack of potatoes. Kevin laughed and squirmed all the way to the kitchen.

"I'd better go save him." Ian followed, giving Melanie a wink as he passed her. "And I don't mean Kevin."

Her head spinning, Melanie stared at the closed kitchen door. She had no idea what she and Kevin were going to do now, or where they would go. But hearing her son's precious laughter from behind that closed door gave her a strength that surprised even her.

"Gabe called me this morning and told me about

your car." Cara set her purse and the pink doughnut box on the dining-room table. The delicious smell of fresh-baked doughnuts filled the room. "Has he replaced the battery yet?"

Melanie shook her head. "The repair shop said they'd deliver it sometime this morning. I tried to tell your brother that I would take care of it myself, but he wouldn't listen to me."

"When Gabe sets his mind to something," Cara said with a grin, "you need a jackhammer to budge him. The only Sinclair more stubborn than Gabe is Lucian."

"Lucian?"

"Believe it or not, there are four Sinclair males." Cara slipped an arm through Melanie's and led her into the living room. "Gabe, of course, he's the oldest. Then Callan, who just got married three months ago, then Lucian, then Reese. You'll meet them sooner or later. For your sake, hope it's later. They can be a little overwhelming."

After meeting Cara and Gabe, Melanie had no doubt that was true. But she wasn't going to be here later, so she would never find out for herself.

"Cara," Melanie said awkwardly. "I'm sorry I'm still here. Your brother already started working on the house this morning, and I'm sure that Kevin and I are in the way."

"Don't be silly. Of course you aren't in the way." Her arm still in Melanie's, Cara pulled her over to the sofa. "I was hoping you and Kevin hadn't left. Here, sit down while I talk to you."

Melanie sat on the edge of the sofa cushion, smoothed her hands nervously over her denim-clad knees. "Talk to me about what?"

"Listen, I know you're anxious to be back on the road, but just hear me out. I have a proposition for you."

"A proposition?"

"I want you to work for the foundation, here at the house. The salary isn't much, but it includes room and board until the house is sold."

Melanie blinked, then furrowed her brow. "I don't understand."

Cara's gaze swept the living room. "This is a big house. Six bedrooms, basement, attic. And it appears that Mildred Witherspoon was a collector. According to Gabe, most of the rooms he looked at last night were jam-packed. And while we're assuming that most of the contents are junk, we still need everything cataloged so we can decide what to do with it all."

"And you want me to do that?" Melanie asked incredulously.

"I wouldn't know where to begin, and wouldn't have time if I did." Cara leaned forward, lowered her voice. "You told me last night that you and Mildred had become long-distance friends through the antique store you worked for. I promised you that I wouldn't tell anyone that, and I'll keep that promise. But you're perfect for this job, Melanie. It could take me days or weeks to find someone else with your qualifications."

Melanie glanced around the large living room. It was hard to tell with just a glance if the antique furniture in the room was valuable or the paintings on the wall were worth more than the price of the frame. It was certainly possible, though. Lots of old country houses contained unknown treasures that had been hidden away, like gold coins buried by a pirate in a secret cove.

She felt her pulse quicken. Even though she'd left the antiques world behind her, it was still in her blood. And every antique dealer dreamed of this kind of an opportunity.

"There would be hundreds of items to sort through and catalog." Melanie shook her head. "Without a computer and Internet link to check items and value, it could take weeks."

"I'll have a computer here tomorrow," Cara said, "and a phone line hooked up immediately. Just say yes."

She wanted to. So badly she could taste it. But it would mean staying in one place, and the thought frightened her.

"I—I can't," Melanie said after a long moment. "It might not be...safe."

Cara put her hand on Melanie's. "Bloomfield County is a small town. No one knows you. You and Kevin will be safe here."

Melanie looked down at Cara's hand on hers. "You don't even know me," Melanie said softly. "How do you know you can trust me?"

"You could have taken anything you wanted last night and left. We'd never have known anything was missing."

"My car broke down," Melanie said wryly. "It's hard to make a getaway on foot with a four-year-old."

Cara shook her head and smiled. "I trust you, Melanie. I also want to help. So does Gabe."

Melanie looked up sharply at the mention of Gabe's name.

"I didn't tell him anything about you," Cara said. "It's up to you to decide what you want him to know. But it's pretty obvious you have a big problem. Though he resists it, it's Gabe's nature to want to take care of everyone. He can be stubborn and difficult, and I've personally wanted to shoot him several times for butting into my business. But he got the family through some rough times after our parents died. If Gabe decides to go to bat for someone, anyone standing in his way had better look out." Cara squeezed Melanie's hand. "You can trust him."

Cara was wrong there, Melanie thought. She couldn't trust anyone. She didn't dare.

But maybe Cara was right about her staying in Bloomfield. No one knew her here. Maybe, just maybe, for a few days, she could work here, give herself a little time to regroup, and come up with a plan. She didn't think Vincent could find her that quickly.

She heard her son laugh again from the kitchen. The past few weeks had been hard on him. He'd like it here, with all this space to run, the same bed to sleep in at night. She'd like that, too.

At Kevin's sudden and loud shriek from the kitchen, Melanie's heart jumped into her throat, but Cara grabbed her arm before she could move. The swinging door from the kitchen into the living room flew open, and Gabe tore through the living room shoving a doughnut into his mouth. Ian was right behind, yelling at him for taking the last maple bar.

Laughing, Kevin ran behind, his face covered with chocolate. They all ran out the front door and pounded down the front steps.

Cara shook her head and frowned. "I knew I

shouldn't have let those doughnuts out of my sight. There's going to be blood if they haven't left any for us."

Melanie stared after the male tornado that had just passed through. She'd never seen anything like it in her life. She'd never had brothers and Phillip, well Phillip had always been so reserved, so...stuffy.

"So what do you say?" Cara asked. "Will you stay?"

Eyes still wide, Melanie turned back to Cara. She hadn't even blinked at the brigade that had just stormed through the house.

Would she stay?

"Why do I get the feeling that Gabe and Lucian don't have an exclusive on stubborn?" Melanie asked.

Cara grinned. "So you'll stay then?"

"Yes." Melanie smiled back at Cara. "I'll stay."

The thick clouds rolled in sometime in the late afternoon. Dark and swollen, they promised rain by nightfall. A chill crept under the doors and through the windowsills into the big house and scurried over the hardwood floors.

Gabe knelt in front of the massive living-room fireplace, dumped the armload of firewood onto the heavy metal grate, then reached up to open the flue. He struck a match, lit the kindling under the wood and blew lightly on it. The flame popped, then flared to life and caught hold.

"I can't remember the last time I saw someone do that."

Startled by Melanie's soft voice, Gabe turned, saw her standing several feet away, her arms folded.

Though he'd spent time playing with Kevin when Cara and Ian had come over, Gabe had stayed upstairs all afternoon and avoided Melanie. Since he'd overheard the phone call she'd made, he'd felt on edge. It annoyed the hell out of him that he was attracted to her, and the fact that she'd gotten under his skin so quickly annoyed him all the more. He needed to keep his distance from her, needed to find his balance again. His control.

Especially now that he'd heard she'd be staying for a while.

He rose slowly, brushed his hands on his jeans. "Since you've seen someone do what?"

"Light a fire like that, without natural gas." She moved closer, in a circular motion, like a wounded animal might approach.

He couldn't figure this woman out. One minute she had that chin of hers stuck up in the air, all bravado, daring anyone to come close, the next minute she was soft and vulnerable. It made him crazy.

"Yeah, well, I'm just full of talent," he said more harshly than he intended, turned to toss another log onto the fire.

He knew he was being a jerk, he just didn't care. Wasn't about to care. He kept his back to her, wondered if she'd left, but then she said, "Kevin's still sleeping. I think you and Ian wore him out this afternoon."

Why was she making small talk like this? he wondered. She'd made it clear that she wanted to be left alone. Obviously she wanted something and couldn't bring herself to just come out and ask. She had to do this little dance. His annoyance had been on simmer all afternoon, now it turned to a full boil.

Thunder rumbled in the distance. He glanced over his shoulder, saw Melanie turn her head toward the sound and frown.

"Why don't you just say whatever's on your mind?" he said tersely. He felt like a complete heel when she stiffened and looked back at him.

"I'm sure Cara told you that Kevin and I will be staying here for a few days," she said coolly.

He nodded. "She told me."

She gazed at the fire, and he saw the flames dancing in her eyes. "We didn't get off on the right foot, but I was hoping that...that we could be friends."

He had no idea why her offer irritated him, or why his mood was as foul as the weather outside. He wasn't being reasonable at all, which only escalated his bad mood.

"Ray might not like it if we were friends," he said dryly.

She glanced up sharply, pressed her lips tightly together. "You listened to my conversation?"

"Not by choice. Next time you call your boyfriend, maybe you should go outside, instead of the laundry room. The vent in there hooks up directly to the upstairs bathroom."

She said nothing, just stared at him, and damn if that chin of hers didn't slide up an inch.

Damn if he didn't want to kiss her.

"So what's the deal, Melanie?" he asked, took a step toward her. "Is he married? Did his wife find out about you, and she's after you with an ax?"

Where the hell was this coming from? Gabe wondered, shocked at himself and the sarcasm that dripped from his words. And why couldn't he stop it?

Her eyes turned to gray ice, narrowed. "Cara

brought enough groceries to feed ten people for a month,'' she said without a hint of emotion in her voice. ''I'm making chicken tonight if you'd care to join us. It should be ready in about an hour. Now if you'll excuse me, I need to go wake my son up.''

She turned smoothly and walked toward the stairs. He wanted to yell at her that they weren't finished talking yet, and she should get her butt right back here.

Thunder rumbled again, closer this time, shaking the windows. He watched her hesitate at the foot of the stairs, saw her hand tighten on the railing, then she glided up the steps with all the grace and poise of a queen.

The hell with this, Gabe thought and tossed another log on the fire. Sparks flew and the flames leaped. He didn't need this aggravation. There was a bar stool at Reese's tavern with his name on it and a mug of beer that fit his hand perfectly. What better way to spend a stormy night than shooting the bull with his brothers and watching a ball game?

No better way, he decided and headed for the back door. No better way at all.

Melanie white-knuckled the blanket and pulled it up to her chin as a clap of thunder shook the bedroom windows. She'd never experienced a ''real'' thunderstorm before. They were rare in Southern California, and the few that did occur were relatively mild and practically over before they began. Unless there was an earthquake, houses didn't shake and windows didn't rattle with the ferocity of the storm that appeared to have settled directly over Mildred Witherspoon's roof.

Lightning lit the dark upstairs bedroom with the power of a two thousand-watt strobe lamp. Biting back a sob, Melanie buried her head under her pillow as the house vibrated from the ensuing thunder.

Beside her, Kevin slept like a rock.

Even as a baby, her son had always been a heavy sleeper, and at this moment, she was especially grateful for that. She would hate for him to see his mother shaking like a mouse under a cat's paw.

Even small, California thunderstorms had always terrified her. And here, in this big, old, pitch-black Victorian farmhouse in Pennsylvania, they absolutely paralyzed her.

Rain pounded the roof; a tree branch too close to the house scratched against the upstairs window. The wind howled.

She wanted to howl, too. Like a baby.

It was only a little past ten. She might as well get up, make some tea, try to read until the storm passed. Anything but lie here, tossing and turning, worrying about the storm one minute, thinking about Gabe the next.

He thought she was having an affair with a married man, which was as ridiculous as it was infuriating. She thought back on her conversation with Raina and realized that it might have sounded that way, but what right did he have to jump to conclusions about her? Who was he to pass judgment on something he knew nothing about?

Teeth clenched, she sat and reached for her navy-blue chenille bathrobe. And besides, why should he care one way or the other what she did?

And why should she care one way or the other what Gabe thought of her?

With a sigh, she sat and pulled her robe on. But she did care. She cared a lot.

Knowing that Gabe thought so little of her hurt. Even after she'd found out that Phillip had been cheating on her with Susan, another stockbroker from his firm, she hadn't considered having an affair, though she had kicked Phillip out of their house for a few days. If she had been stronger, she never would have let him back in.

But Kevin had been only six weeks old at the time. Her delivery had been difficult, and her recovery took longer than expected. She had no parents to help, and Phillip had driven away the few casual friendships she'd had. She'd had nowhere to go, no money of her own. With Kevin as her priority, she'd stayed.

And she'd been faithful. She'd believed in the sanctity of marriage, even though her husband hadn't. She might have forgiven him one affair, but then came Stephanie. Melanie hadn't even asked Phillip where he'd met her, she'd simply packed her and eight-month-old Kevin's things and moved out with what little money she'd been hoarding.

Phillip had been furious she'd left him—how dare she treat him that way after everything he'd given her? he'd yelled at her. That was the first time he'd struck her, and she had vowed she'd never give him another chance.

Until Louise showed up. Tears streaming down her perfectly made-up face, every strand of silver hair perfectly in place, her mother-in-law had pleaded with Melanie to come back to her son. She'd already arranged for therapy. She'd promised things would be better. A boy needs his father, Louise had said. Phillip was behaving so badly because he was grieving the recent loss of his own father. Families stayed together always, Louise had said, no matter what.

So Melanie had given in and gone back, hopeful that the therapy would make a difference. And for the next year, it had seemed to.

Then she found the notes from Kathy and confronted him. This time when he'd hit her, she knew she would never go back. She and Kevin would make it on their own. She'd filed for divorce, but Phillip refused to sign any papers. He'd hired his high-price Beverly Hills lawyers to fight her, but she'd hung in. Ten days before their divorce would have been final, Phillip was killed in a boating accident.

Melanie knew that Louise still blamed her for Phillip's death. She'd pretended to be sweet and loving, had even persuaded her and Kevin to move in with her for a while, then doted on both of them, when all along what she'd really wanted was to take Kevin away, to punish her daughter-in-law and claim her grandson to replace the son she'd lost.

The nightmare should have ended with Phillip's death, but in fact, it had only begun.

Let Gabe Sinclair think whatever he wanted, she thought, hugging herself tightly. Kevin was all that mattered to her. All that *could* matter to her.

At the flash of lightning, Melanie jumped, then pulled her robe tightly over her white boxer pajamas and squeezed her eyes shut, waiting for the thunder to stop shaking the house. When it finally passed, she glanced at Kevin again. He hadn't even budged. Shaking her head, she smiled at her son, reached to brush a strand of hair off his forehead.

And froze at the sound of a door closing downstairs.

She reached for the lamp beside the bed and pulled the chain. Nothing happened. It had worked only fifteen minutes ago, when she'd turned it off. She moved quickly to the other side of the bed and tried the other lamp. It didn't work, either.

The power was out.

Her heart pounded furiously as she rushed to the bedroom door and opened it a few inches, listening, waiting. She heard nothing other than the storm now.

It had to be her imagination. Her frightened mind playing tricks on her. But she couldn't stay up here, wondering if someone was downstairs. She had to know, had to see that everything was all right.

She closed the bedroom door behind her, then quietly inched her way down the hall and the stairs. The darkness engulfed her, and the sound of the rain pummeling the porch roof echoed in the living room.

She went still at another sound, a muffled squeak coming from the kitchen.

A loose shutter, she told herself. Maybe a mouse or a rat. She shuddered at the thought, but prayed that's all it was. It had to be. Vincent couldn't have found her here. It couldn't be him.

Please don't let it be him.

The hardwood floor was cold on her bare feet, and her hands shook as she moved slowly toward the kitchen. The air felt colder to her when she stepped inside, but she could see that the back door was closed. *Thank God,* she released the breath she'd been holding, then froze as she stepped in a puddle of cold water.

Even in the darkness, she could see the gleam of water trailing from the back door, across the kitchen floor and leading to…the open basement door.

The fuse boxes were down there. And so was whoever had trailed water across the floor.

They'd also have to come out again, she realized.

Drawing in a long, shaky breath, she reached for the cast-iron frying pan she'd washed this morning and set back on the stove. Her knees felt like warm rubber as she crept across the kitchen and waited. Her heart hammered in her chest.

She heard the sound of footsteps moving up the stairs, saw a faint beam of light. She lifted the frying pan with both hands.

The footsteps were heavy, almost to the top of the stairs. When the beam of light hit the floor in front of her, she swung the frying pan like a baseball bat, made solid contact with a hard, muscular body. She heard his grunt of pain, the earthy swearword.

Lightning flashed as she raised her arms to swing again.

Gabe!

His face was twisted in pain, and he teetered at the top of the basement stairs, his hands clutching the doorjamb. The frying pan clattered to the floor as she reached out and grabbed him before he fell backward.

"Ohmigod, Gabe, I'm so sorry!"

He slumped into her arms, gasping for breath, and she bore the brunt of his weight as she led him into the living room. His clothes and hair were wet, and she felt the dampness seep through her robe. She held him tightly against her, guided him to the sofa in front of the fireplace, and he collapsed onto the cushions with a soft moan.

Oh, dear Lord, what had she done!

The fire he'd built earlier had died, but the embers still glowed a warm orange and cast a soft light into the room. She pushed the fire screen aside and threw two more logs inside, then replaced the screen and hurried back to Gabe. He lay with his head back and his eyes closed, and she thought maybe he'd passed out. Thank God he was breathing!

"Gabe, can you hear me? Are you all right?"

He didn't answer, and she ran her hands over his dark hair and felt the wetness, but it appeared to be water, not blood. She touched his face, felt the light stubble of an evening beard, then opened his denim jacket. It was soaked, so she tugged it off, no thanks to him, and laid her palms on his broad chest. She felt the heavy beating of his heart, felt the warmth of his body through the soft flannel shirt he wore.

The fire crackled to life behind her, lighting up the room.

"Gabe." She brought her face close to his. "Wake up. Please wake up."

He opened his eyes slowly.

Relief poured through her. Thank God, he hadn't passed out. "Talk to me," she said softly. "Where did I hit you?"

He covered her hands with his.

"Your chest? I hit you in the chest?"

He nodded.

She brushed his hands away and unbuttoned his shirt, gasped at the bright welt she saw through the sprinkling of dark, coarse hair. Tenderly she touched her fingertips to his chest. His skin was hot, his muscles like steel. She stared, tried to remind herself that she'd injured the man, and she certainly shouldn't be ogling him. Heat crept up through her fingers, her arms, then pooled low in her belly.

She pulled her hands away, but he took them and

put them back. "That feels good," he murmured roughly.

It certainly did, she thought. Too damn good. And not the kind of good she'd intended. Her skin suddenly felt tight and hot, her breasts achy. And still she couldn't remove her hands from his skin. He had the smell of the storm on him, and his own masculine scent that stirred her insides.

"What were you doing down in the basement?" she whispered, trying desperately to hold onto reality.

"Turning...power...back on."

The storm raged outside, and a roll of thunder made her press closer to him, hold tighter. "Why did you come back?"

"To apologize...for being a jackass." His gaze dropped to her mouth. "I'm sorry."

She had no idea when her robe had come undone, and it hardly seemed to matter at the moment. Her body was flush with his, her breasts pressed against his solid chest, one long curvy leg lined up with his. She was practically lying on top of him.

God help her, still she couldn't move.

It felt like slow motion, like a dream. Her limbs were heavy, her body drugged. She supposed it was an aftereffect of all the adrenaline she'd had pumping through her only minutes before, but it hardly mattered. Only the warm, safe feel of Gabe's body under hers mattered.

It had been so long since she'd felt safe, even longer since she'd felt desire.

"Melanie," he said raggedly, "God, I'm so sorry."

"Sorry?" she repeated dimly. "For earlier?"

"No. For now."

His mouth swooped up and caught hers. Consumed her. She didn't know when she'd ever felt such intense passion from someone else, or from herself. But she clung to him, her emotions raw and wild and out of control. His arms came around her, dragged her against him, while his lips devoured her hungrily. She answered, as greedy as him, raked her hands over his chest, his face, his scalp.

He moaned deep in his throat, slid his hands under her pajama top, covered her breasts with his large, rough hands. She sucked in a breath at his touch, wanted those hands on her, everywhere, at the same time.

The lightning struck again, only this time, with the thunder came reality. What was she thinking? How could she be doing this? Making love with a stranger!

Gasping, she pulled away, tugged her robe tightly around her and eased away from Gabe. His eyes were glazed and confused as he looked at her. He sighed heavily and dropped his head back against the sofa.

The fire crackled behind them.

"I—I'm sorry. That was my fault." She rose from the sofa on wobbly knees. "But it was a mistake. It can't happen again."

"Melanie—"

He started to reach for her, but she backed away. "It can't, Gabe. I'm only going to be here for a few days. In spite of what you think of me, this really isn't something that I do."

"Dammit, Melanie," Gabe ground out. "I know that. I was angry earlier, frustrated because you won't let me help you."

"You can't help," she whispered. "No one can."

"I don't believe that," he said tightly.

"It doesn't matter what you believe. I'm not going to lie and tell you that I didn't enjoy what just happened between us, because I did. But you have to promise that it won't happen again. If it does, I'll have to leave."

He opened his mouth, but she shook her head. "Promise me."

Eyes narrowed, he pressed his lips tightly together. "Fine."

She relaxed then, drew in a deep breath. "I've got to get back to Kevin. Good night."

She had already started for the stairs when she stopped suddenly, then slowly turned back around.

"Rae is a friend of mine, Gabe," she said softly. "A woman friend, as in Raina."

She turned again, but not before she saw his eyes close, not before she heard him sigh.

"Melanie."

She hesitated at the base of the stairs and looked over her shoulder.

"I lied." He stared at her, the light of the fire dancing in his dark eyes. "I'm not sorry about kissing you."

Her hand tightened on the banister. She could go back to him, forget her brave little speech about how it could never happen again and for just one night let herself feel.

And hate herself in the morning. She drew in a slow breath to give herself strength, wished to God that she could have met this man under different circumstances.

But she hadn't, and nothing in the world could change that.

"I'm going to be here a few more days," she said

evenly. "It will be easier for both of us to just forget about this."

His eyes narrowed. "Can you?"

"Yes," she lied.

The fire played on the hard angles of his face as he watched her. "I'll let myself out in a little while, when the storm eases up."

She nodded, then turned and hurried back upstairs before she changed her mind.

"It's been six weeks, Vincent."

Louise Van Camp lifted her cold, imperious gaze from the fluffy white poodle on her lap and looked sharply at Vincent. Her long, sleek sheath was Christian Dior, stark white, a sharp contrast against the royal-blue velvet sofa where she sat as straight and stiff as one of the polished silver candlesticks on the living-room mantel.

"Yes, ma'am." Vincent's impulse had been to tell the old biddy that he not only knew how to count days, but he could even tell the time, too. But, as always, he'd bit back his first impulse and taken the more diplomatic route. Louise paid him too much money for him to tell her what he really thought of her snobby airs and holier-than-thou attitude. The woman had never worked a day in her life. Her husband had been a stinkin' rich, influential judge, and when the old geezer kicked the bucket, she'd become a stinkin' rich widow who thought she was better than everybody else.

He hated the old bat, but he loved her money.

"And what, pray tell," Louise said coolly, "besides buying new clothes and bothering my maids, have you been doing to earn the obscene amount of money I pay you?''

Vincent took in the huge diamonds sparkling on Louise's wrinkled hands and earlobes, the solid gold ashtray on the coffee table that she refused to let anyone use, the ruby-and-diamond collar on that stupid mutt of hers. And she thought that what she paid *him* was obscene? He ground his back teeth together, careful to keep his expression calm and concerned, and once again went with the second, more sensible reply.

''I've been monitoring all of Melissa's old contacts,'' he said evenly. ''Especially in the antique business. I also have a man watching that friend of hers, Raina Williams, now Raina Sarbanes. We'll know immediately if she turns up there.''

It had taken a little digging to find the Sarbanes woman, but door-to-door inquiries of Melissa's high school friends had all come back to the name Raina Williams. More digging had traced the woman to Greece, where she'd married and divorced, then to Italy, and now she was in Boston. It had been a long, intensive, as well as expensive search, but worth it. It appeared that Melissa and Raina had not seen each other in years, and though it was a long shot that they had reconnected, Vincent was leaving no stone unturned. If there was any chance that Melissa would show up at her old friend's door, then they'd be waiting for her.

Louise pressed her thin lips together and stroked her dog's head. ''Six weeks and that's all you've got? This Raina woman?''

Vincent carefully reminded himself to breathe slowly. There was too much at stake to blow the sweet deal he had going with the Van Camp broad.

He'd take his anger out later on someone else. He thought of that cute little cocktail waitress at the Kitty Kat Lounge who'd been giving him the eye. Maybe it was time for the two of them to get…close.

That thought composed him enough to calmly continue. "I'm working on establishing a contact in the Boston phone company," he said in his best reassuring tone. "If the women have made any calls to each other, then we should be able to track her down from the Sarbanes's woman's phone records."

"I don't like the sound of the word 'should,' Vincent. I'm not paying you for 'should.' I want results." Louise narrowed her cold eyes. "I want my grandson."

"Yes, ma'am." He dropped his gaze respectfully, but inside, his stomach twisted with fury.

For every "Yes, ma'am" that he was forced to placate Louise with, for every "I'm sorry, Mrs. Van Camp," Vincent intended to make Melissa pay dearly.

His blood heated at the thought, his palms itched. His groin tightened and swelled.

This time when he found the bitch, and he would find her, he would teach her a lesson she would never forget. As long as Louise had her grandson back, Vincent doubted that the old woman would care what happened to her daughter-in-law.

He planned on a long, slow, let's-get-to-know-each-other with Melissa when he brought her back. And if she fought, so much the better. He liked a woman who resisted. Tears and pleading made him feel strong and powerful. Virile.

Afraid that he would become visibly aroused, Vincent snapped his attention back to Louise. "I'll find

Melissa and your grandson, Mrs. Van Camp. I promise.''

''See that you do,'' she said with a sniff. ''And be quick about it. A new semester starts at the academy just after the first of the year. Every male Van Camp has attended that school for the past fifty years, and I intend for Kevin to be there as well.''

''Yes, ma'am.''

''You may go now.''

''Yes, ma'am.''

Vincent backed away, then turned, narrowing his eyes. The need to smash something overwhelmed him. Anger and frustration squeezed his chest like a vise.

Melissa had been smart this time. Very smart. But she'd trip up somewhere, make a mistake, and then he'd find her. He'd had a soft spot for her, he knew. Those big gray eyes of hers and that killer body had clouded his thinking. He'd been too gentle with her the last time he'd brought her back from Northern California, too forgiving. She obviously hadn't taken him seriously when he'd told her she better behave.

She would this time, he thought with a slow smile. This time when he found her, he wouldn't be gentle and he wouldn't be forgiving.

Chapter 5

Gabe opened his eyes at seven-thirty the next morning, then slammed them shut again with a groan as he realized he'd fallen asleep on the sofa. Damn. Last thing he remembered he'd been staring into the fire, listening to the rain on the roof.

Waiting for his body to calm down after that mistake—as Melanie had called it.

A mistake that contained all the heat and power of a lightning bolt. He wouldn't be surprised if his eyebrows were singed.

And she wanted him to forget about it.

Sure he would. When snowshoes became the fashion in hell.

He sat slowly, rubbed his hands over his face, then raked his fingers through his hair. With a groan, he cranked his neck to the left, then to the right, until it gave a good, solid crack. Much better, he thought, then winced as he rubbed his chest. Thank God she hadn't hit him a few inches higher with that frying pan. He'd have had a broken nose for sure, instead of just the wind knocked out of him.

But then, those lips of hers had packed quite a wallop as well. He wasn't sure which was more lethal, her mouth or that cast-iron pan.

The smell of bacon frying seeped through the fog of sleep in his brain, and he dragged the incredible smell deep into his lungs. Obviously Melanie was already up, and he couldn't help but wonder if she'd gotten any more sleep last night than he had. His pride hoped like hell she hadn't.

Shaking his head, he glanced down at the socks on his feet, then remembered he'd left his muddy boots on the porch when he'd come in from the storm last night and found the power had gone out. He also realized his shirt was still unbuttoned. The memory of Melanie's soft hands on his chest, her fingertips sliding over his skin, made his jaw tighten.

He narrowed a glance at the kitchen door. Forget about last night?

Right.

Buttoning his shirt, he headed for the kitchen, found Melanie at the counter, cracking eggs into a clear glass bowl. Butter sizzled in a frying pan on the stove, and he heard the sound of running water coming from the downstairs bathroom. Kevin was singing a tune from that kid's show about purple dinosaurs.

"Morning."

She turned at his gravelly greeting, and based on the rise of color on her cheeks, it appeared she hadn't forgotten about last night, either. Small satisfaction, but right now, he'd take whatever he could get.

"Morning." She glanced quickly away. "Coffee's ready."

A large black mug sat beside the coffeepot, and he helped himself to a cup, then leaned against the counter, watching her. She must have showered already, he thought, taking in the damp ends of her shiny, dark hair that fell in soft waves around the collar of her deep blue blouse. His gaze skimmed down her back to where her black jeans hugged the curve of her bottom and long slender legs.

He'd seen a great deal of that curvy body last night under her robe, touched her smooth, silky skin and full breasts. He felt a sharp twist in his gut.

She was right. He *did* need to forget.

"I fell asleep on the sofa." He'd be damned if he'd apologize for it, either.

She merely nodded, dumped the eggs into the frying pan, where they bubbled and popped. "Not the most comfortable night you've spent, I'm sure."

No, he thought, but that had nothing to do with the sofa. He shrugged. "I've had worse."

She arched one brow, reached for a pepper shaker. "Oh?"

"The bench in Reese's tavern after an all-night celebration of my brother Callan and Abby's marriage was hardly a night at the Ritz," he said, still not quite sure how he'd ended up twisted on that booth seat. But it had been a great party, that much he remembered. He smiled at the memory. "That was three months ago, and I've still got a kink in my knee."

Melanie smiled, and Gabe tried not to think about what her soft mouth had felt like against his last night.

"Then there was the all-nighter in Lucian's sports car," he continued. "A seven-year-old would have been cramped in that little two-seater, let alone two six-foot-four men.''

She looked at him, questioning.

''We were taking turns sleeping and watching Cara's apartment in Philly,'' he explained. ''She'd been a private investigator at the time, and there'd been a couple of attempts on her life. We just wanted to make sure we were around if there were any more.''

Her eyes widened with surprise. ''Someone wanted to kill Cara?''

He nodded. ''Turned out to be Ian's cousin, but that's another story for another time. How about you?'' He took a sip of hot coffee, leveled his gaze at her and carefully asked, ''You ever slept in a car?''

His question wasn't subtle, nor had he intended it to be. She stilled, then reached for the spatula on the stove and flipped the eggs.

''Melanie.'' He moved closer, tightened his hand around the mug in his hand. ''I'm sorry, but I need to know.''

She looked up at him, and he saw the wariness in her gray eyes. If a man wasn't careful, he could lose himself in those eyes. He had to remind himself to be careful. Very careful.

''Why?'' she asked softly. ''Why do you need to know anything about me and my son? Why does it matter to you?''

''It beats the hell out of me,'' he said honestly, then reached up and touched her jaw with his fingertips. She stiffened, but didn't pull away. ''I just do, and it just does.''

He felt the warm breath of her sigh on his hand,

tried to ignore the bullet of desire that shot straight through his body.

"Kevin and I haven't been sleeping in the car, nor have we missed any meals," she said quietly, then smiled as she eased away from him. "We're fine, Gabe. Really we are."

"Like hell you are," he said, but without accusation. "You've got a problem, lady. And pretending it doesn't exist won't make it go away."

"No one knows better than I do what exists and doesn't exist in my life. But I believe that's my concern, not yours." She picked up a plate on the stove, scooped the cooked eggs onto it. "Breakfast is just about ready, and I'm sure you'd like to use the bathroom and wash up."

"Melanie—"

"And since it was you who created the monster," she said lightly as she turned toward the kitchen table, "why don't you go in there and see if you can drag Kevin away from washing his hands. He's been at it for the past ten minutes and—"

"Something sure smells good," a deep, male voice said from the back door. "Hope you've got extra."

With a squeak, Melanie whirled at the sound of the man's voice. The plate in her hand fell to the floor and shattered.

Lucian looked down at the mess and winced. "Guess not."

"Dammit, Lucian, do you have to sneak up on people like that?" Gabe snapped.

"I knocked on the front door and there was no answer, so I came around the back." Lucian's gaze swung back to Melanie, and his smile was contrite. "Sorry I scared you."

He'd done more than scare her, Gabe thought. He'd terrified her. Her face had gone pale, and her eyes were wide with fear. What the hell was going on with this woman?

Someone *was* after her. He felt it in his gut. Someone who wanted to hurt her. Why else would she act this way?

His jaw tightened at the thought. He couldn't ask, not now. She'd back away for sure, maybe even run if he pushed.

But he'd find out. One way or another, by God, he'd find out.

Melanie blinked then, and a bright pink rushed in to color her white cheeks. "No, I—I'm sorry," she stammered. "You just startled me, that's all."

She bent toward the floor at the same time Gabe did, and their knees bumped. She steadied herself with a hand on his thigh, then quickly pulled her fingers away and gathered the larger pieces of broken plate.

"You must be Melanie." Lucian grabbed a roll of paper towels from the counter and picked his way through the jagged pieces of plate and smooshed egg. "Gabe told us that you and your son are staying here."

"Just for a few days," she said carefully, "while I catalog the contents of the house."

"We'll take care of this." Gabe took the broken pieces of plate from her hand, ignored the burning sensation left by her touch on his thigh only a moment ago.

She hesitated, then nodded. "I'll get some more eggs started while the pan's still hot." Melanie stood, then looked at Lucian and smiled. "Over easy all right with you?"

Much to Gabe's annoyance, Lucian grinned. "Any way they turn out is just fine by me."

"Was there something you wanted, Lucian?" Gabe wrapped the bulk of the mess in several paper towels, then dumped the lumpy bundle in Lucian's hands. "Besides a meal?"

Lucian's grin widened. "The painting crew will be here in an hour. Just thought I'd double-check the supply list you gave me last night."

Gabe frowned at his brother. He knew exactly why Lucian had come over here. It had nothing to do with supply lists or painting crews and everything to do with a certain dark-haired mystery woman. Last night, at the tavern, Gabe had casually mentioned Melanie and Kevin to his brothers. They would have found out soon enough anyway, and it would have looked strange if he hadn't told them that the woman and her son were staying here for a while.

But what *was* strange to Gabe was that he hadn't *wanted* to tell his brothers about her. He hadn't wanted them coming around the house. Which was ridiculous, of course, Gabe knew. Even though he was in charge of the Witherspoon project, both Callan and Lucian would be involved from time to time. And Reese would be by just because he was nosy. The idea of a single woman in town whom he hadn't put the make on yet would be too much of a challenge to resist.

But ridiculous or not, it didn't seem to matter. He still didn't like it.

And he sure as hell didn't like the look in Lucian's eyes at the moment. Gabe had seen that same look zero in on more than one unsuspecting female. It just had never bothered him before. He'd never taken it...personally before.

"Hey, bro." Brows raised, Lucian glanced down at the socks on Gabe's feet. "Better watch where you step."

Gabe narrowed a look at his brother. "I was just going to say the same to you, Luc."

Lucian's grin split his face. "I'll finish up here while you go wash up. I've got a comb and razor in the truck if you need them. You look a little...rumpled this morning."

From his wrinkled clothes, messed hair and morning beard, there was no doubt that Lucian had figured out he'd spent the night here. Gabe would straighten his brother out about that later. He sure as hell didn't want Lucian or anyone else thinking that he'd slept anywhere but the sofa.

He glanced at Melanie who was busy cracking eggs into a bowl. Leaving her alone with Lucian was like leaving a lamb with a wolf. He sent his brother another look of warning, but Lucian just kept grinning like a damn fool.

He would strangle him later, Gabe decided and followed the sound of Barney's theme song coming from the bathroom.

Melanie stared out the front window, watching Gabe and Lucian talk beside the black pickup parked in the front driveway. Lucian was smiling about something, but Gabe seemed irritated, kept shaking his head and frowning darkly.

Good heavens, but they were two stunning examples of masculinity. She couldn't help but wonder about the other two brothers, Reese and Callan, if they were as handsome as Lucian and Gabe. She was surprised that only one Sinclair male—Callan—had been snagged into the web of matrimony. No doubt it wasn't due to lack of effort on the part of Bloomfield County females, Melanie thought. She imagined that the women here had to take a ticket just to get in line for a chance with one of the Sinclair males.

She still couldn't believe that she'd reacted the way she had when Lucian had walked into the kitchen and caught her off guard. He must think her a complete idiot, squeaking like she had and dropping that plate. But she'd thought, for one heart-stopping, horrifying moment, that he was Vincent.

Not that Lucian looked anything like Vincent. Vincent was shorter than Lucian, his hair longer and always worn slicked back, like black patent leather. Vincent's skin was also darker and more coarse. But her nerves were shot. She was on edge, not only from the storm last night, but also because of what had happened between her and Gabe.

No one had ever kissed her like that before.

And she had never kissed anyone back like that, either.

It had taken her a long time to fall asleep after she'd gone back to bed, long after the thunder and lightning had stopped, long after the rain had ceased. She'd felt as if the storm had moved into her body, rolling and crashing around, pounding away at her insides.

Making her want things she couldn't have.

Lying there in the darkness, she'd known Gabe was downstairs, that all she had to do was go to him and he would ease the ache inside her. If only for a little while, he could make her forget.

How easy that would have been. To make love with a stranger, to know that there would be no involvement beyond the physical. There would be nothing beyond the need. Nothing but pleasure.

But she wasn't that naïve. She understood at some very primitive level there was more than simple lust between her and Gabe. There was some strange connection. And that was what had stopped her. Because she couldn't allow that, couldn't allow herself to feel that way about him or any other man. Not now, maybe not ever.

"Mommy." Kevin tugged at her leg. "Can I play with Batman now?"

Turning away from the window, she scooped her son up in her arms and squeezed him until he laughed. "Of course you can, sweetheart. But you have to give me a kiss first."

He rolled his eyes, then wrapped his short little arms around her neck, puckered up and gave her a big smack on her lips. "*Now* can I play?"

She hugged him again, then set him down, and he ran upstairs to the bedroom where he'd built a pretend Gotham City with his action figures and Batmobile.

He'd been quiet during breakfast, his blue eyes darting back and forth from Gabe to Lucian as they'd talked about the ball game last night and the painting crew, but he hadn't seemed frightened. Since that incident four months ago, when Kevin had seen Vincent back her against the door in her apartment in Northern California, then "strongly encourage" her to move back into Louise's house in Beverly Hills, Kevin had seemed to be afraid of men.

Until they'd come here. Kevin wasn't afraid of Gabe or Ian, and he seemed fine with Lucian, too. In just the few days they'd been here, her son was much more like the happy, rambunctious little boy he'd been before Louise had forced her way into their lives and turned everything upside down.

At the sound of trucks pulling up in the front driveway, Melanie felt a knot tighten in her stomach. When she moved back to the window, she saw Gabe approach two pickups loaded with ladders and tarps and paint. If she was going to stay here, she knew she was going to have to get used to strangers coming and going.

She watched Gabe as he pointed at the house and gave directions to three men. Slowly the knot in her stomach eased. Somehow, knowing that Gabe would be here, she felt safer, that she and Kevin would be fine.

Just a few days, she told herself. A week or two at the most. Then she'd have to move on. With Vincent looking for her, staying in one place too long might be dangerous. Because he'd find her. She was certain of that. Vincent was not the kind of man to give up.

But she wouldn't think about Vincent now. Wouldn't think about where he was or what he was doing. Or what he would do if he found her. It would make her crazy if she did.

And besides, she thought, turning away from the window and moving back into the living room, she had a job to do here. A big job.

Mildred Witherspoon's house was approximately four thousand square feet, not including the attic space or basement. Six bedrooms upstairs, two full bathrooms—a large one upstairs, a small one downstairs—kitchen, dining room, living room and parlor. Every room seemed to be packed with a lifetime of "stuff."

An opportunity to explore a house like this was a dream come true for any antique dealer. She felt like a child on Christmas morning, surrounded by a mountain of brightly wrapped presents.

Palms itching, she pulled the slipcover off the sofa in front of the fireplace. Standard 1940s design, a deep burgundy flossed fabric. Still in remarkable shape, but nothing to get excited about.

Until she remembered last night, lying on this very sofa in Gabe's arms. Kissing him. Him kissing her, his hands on her skin. On her breasts. The memory made her pulse speed up.

She sat on the edge of the sofa and ran her fingers over the coarse texture of the fabric, felt the hard lumps in the cushions. When she'd come down the stairs this morning and found him asleep out here, his long, powerful legs draped over one end, his strong, muscular arms hanging from the other, she'd felt a twist in her stomach. He hadn't looked nearly so serious in his sleep. If anything, he'd looked calm, younger somehow, and she'd had an urge to brush his hair off his forehead as she would do to Kevin.

But she hadn't, of course. Even the slightest touch would be a dangerous thing. Just this morning, when she'd accidentally brushed her hand against his hard, muscled thigh, she'd felt her pulse skip. Her fingers still felt warm from the heat his skin had radiated through his jeans.

The front door opened, and he walked in. His gaze met hers, dropped to the sofa, then slowly lifted again. She knew he was thinking about last night, the same as she was. She felt the heat of her blush on her cheeks.

"The painters will be here for a few days," he said evenly, holding her gaze with his. "They'll be outside, but they may need to use the bathroom or speak to me occasionally."

"If I'm in the way, you can—"

Frowning, he shook his head. "You won't be. I just didn't want you to be—" he hesitated "—surprised."

He meant *scared,* she thought, disgusted with herself that she'd acted like such a frightened little mouse this morning when Lucian had unexpectedly walked in. Gabe was probably afraid she'd be breaking things every time she turned around.

Lifting her chin, she held her eyes steady with his. "I'll be fine. Don't worry about me."

"I'll be working in the upstairs bathroom. If you need anything, just let me know."

"Thanks."

With a nod, he moved up the stairs. She watched him until he moved out of sight, then she glanced back down at the sofa.

If you need anything, just let me know.

A shiver ran through her at his words.

If only she could.

With a sigh, she turned her attention to the job at hand and got to work.

The bathtub plumbing proved to be as difficult as the sink. Gabe remembered to keep his language in check, but it took him over an hour to replace the corroded steel pipe with new copper fittings, then another hour just to remove the rusted fixtures. It probably would have taken him less time if Kevin hadn't popped in a couple of times, once just to see what all the pounding was about, and once to show him the neat missile launcher on his toy Batmobile. With the press of a button, the sponge missile shot six feet up in the air.

And straight down into the open drain of the bathtub.

Fortunately a two-foot-long spring-loaded hose with a claw at the end saved the day, and Gabe became an instant hero in Kevin's eyes.

They both agreed that Kevin's mother didn't need to know about the rescue.

He hadn't seen her all morning, though he had heard her come up the stairs and check on her son a couple of times. He'd also heard her speaking to Russell, the foreman on the painting crew. Gabe had almost gone downstairs then, just to check that everything was all right, but decided against it. If she needed his help with anything, she'd just have to ask. He wasn't about to hover around, waiting for her to come to him. He would probably be an old man before that would happen, anyway. Besides, he had work to do, and it wouldn't get done thinking about her.

Since she was staying for a few days, they would be spending a lot of time together in the house. It would be a hell of a lot easier on both of them if he kept to himself and she did the same. Shoot, this was a big house. It wouldn't be that difficult to stay out of her way.

And since he'd made a promise that he wouldn't kiss her again, he knew he'd better keep his distance.

Because all he could think about was kissing her again.

The only problem was, he was thinking about a whole hell of a lot more than just kissing.

The next few days were definitely going to be...uncomfortable.

Well, dammit, why should he tiptoe around the house, worrying that he might run into her? So he was attracted to her. So what? She certainly wasn't the first—and she sure as hell wouldn't be the last—woman he ever kissed. Big deal. If she could forget about it, then so could he.

He tossed his wrench into his toolbox, scrubbed his hands, then headed down to the kitchen. He was hungry, and if he wanted to go to the kitchen and find something to eat, then that's what he would do, dammit.

Halfway down the stairs, he saw her and stopped. She knelt beside a stained glass lamp sitting on an antique desk behind the sofa, a dreamy expression on her face.

His throat went dry as he watched her gently run her fingertips over the colorful yellow and dark green glass on the lamp.

When she glanced up and saw him watching her, he expected her expression to change, for her to retreat behind the mask of cautious indifference she normally wore.

But she didn't. Instead she did something that equally surprised him.

She smiled.

A bright, genuine smile that reached her gray eyes and lit up her entire face.

The tightness in his throat nearly cut off his

breathing. Dammit, he should have stayed upstairs, after all.

"Gabe." She practically whispered his name. "Come here, you have to see this."

With the look she was giving him, he would have gone over there and done a triple somersault if she'd asked him to.

He moved beside her, knelt down, forced his attention to the lamp she so lovingly stroked.

"It's a Tiffany," she said reverently.

"Yeah?" He knew that. Everyone knew these were called Tiffany lamps.

"No, it's a *real* Tiffany. Bronze base and leaded glass." She touched one delicate yellow flower design. "There were hundreds of thousands of reproductions, but this one is not only an original, it's signed. It's old, probably around the turn-of-the-century. And it's in perfect condition."

"I take it that's good?"

She looked at him, startled, then gave a dry laugh. "Good? My Lord, it's better than good. And look at this desk." She ran her hand over the unusual swirled grain of the desk front. "It's solid Crotch Mahogany, probably from the early nineteenth century. Very rare for this wood to be solid. It was almost always used as a veneer. Even the brass handles are the originals, which is even more rare."

He had to tear his eyes away from her so he could look. It just looked like an old desk to him. A nice one, maybe, but nothing to get all dewy-eyed over.

"There's more," she said breathlessly. "They'll have to be authenticated, but those paintings are also nineteenth century. Broome, Cooke, Thornley. And that's just this one room. There's no telling what we'll find upstairs or in the attic or basement.''

Her eyes were bright, her face flushed with excitement, her lips softly parted. He was only inches from her. He could smell the faint floral scent that drifted from her skin. His insides cinched and twisted, and the hunger he'd felt earlier had nothing to do with the hunger that filled him now.

He stood, took a step back and shoved his hands into the front pockets of his jeans before he broke his promise not to kiss her. He looked around the room at all the furniture and paintings and miscellaneous lamps and knickknacks. Before, he'd thought it was all junk, just a bunch of old stuff, but Melanie seemed to know what she was talking about.

In fact, she was quite knowledgeable, now that he thought about it.

He glanced back at her. ''This is your business, isn't it?'' he asked her pointedly. ''What you do.''

Her smiled slowly faded. ''Was, what I used to do. Not anymore.''

''And that's how you knew Mildred, wasn't it?''

''Yes,'' she said quietly. ''She bought a few small things from the antique dealer I used to work for. Mostly china and a few small silver items. I handled her account.''

The light had faded from her eyes, and suddenly Gabe wanted to kick himself for asking. Dammit, anyway, why couldn't he have kept his big mouth shut and just let her enjoy herself for a few minutes? He felt like he'd just kicked a puppy.

He'd think about this new information later, he decided. Much later. Right now he wanted to see that smile of hers again.

He forced a light tone and grinned, looking around the room once again. "So what now?"

The brilliance returned to her eyes. "You mean you don't know?"

He shook his head.

Her smile lit up the room. "We have an auction."

Chapter 6

In Bloomfield County, Squire's Inn and Tavern was *the* place to have a cold one and the "best darn pepperoni pizza known to man," according to the carved wood sign outside. Reese Sinclair, owner and proprietor, and the youngest Sinclair male at thirty-one, also boasted his establishment made the "best darn hamburgers, too." Since Melanie had already sampled one of those hamburgers her first night at the Witherspoon house and agreed with Reese's assertion, she was looking forward to the pizza.

Cara had taken Kevin to look at a suit of armor standing guard by the bathrooms, and except for the jukebox in the corner currently playing Tom Petty and the Heartbreakers' *Free Falling,* everything about the tavern was eighteenth century English: tudor design, dark woods, heavy oak beams, peg and groove floor.

The room was large and masculine, charming, very much like the men surrounding her at this very moment: Gabe on her right, Lucian on her left, Ian directly across.

She felt absolutely overwhelmed.

She still wasn't quite certain how she'd let herself be talked into this "celebration" as Gabe had called it. One minute she'd been talking about an auction, and the next thing she knew, Gabe had called Cara and told her to round everybody up and meet them at the tavern at seven o'clock.

It made her nervous to be out like this, in a public place, with so many other people around, but at the same time, it also made her feel alive. She hadn't even realized until this moment how long it had been since she'd been with other adults, laughing and having a good time. How much she missed it.

"Hey there, gorgeous, you come here often?" Reese Sinclair winked at her as he set a pitcher of frothy beer and carafe of dark red wine on the table. "How 'bout you ditch these morons and come out with me?"

While Gabe glared darkly at Reese and Lucian told him that he'd seen her first, Melanie blushed at the brothers' outrageous flirting. If there was one thing that the Sinclair brothers were not, it was shy. And based on the longing looks from some of the ladies in the room, they weren't at a loss for female companionship, either. No big surprise there.

One woman in particular, Melanie noted, a petite, pretty redhead in tight black pants and a scoop-necked fuchsia tank top, had locked her gaze on Gabe since the moment he'd walked into the tavern. Melanie was certain that if looks could kill, she'd be laid out flat right now holding a bunch of lilies. Gabe had nodded and smiled at the woman, but he hadn't gone over to say hello, which had seemed to aggravate the redhead all the more. And though Melanie knew she had no right to feel the way she did, she couldn't stop the warm ripple of pleasure inside her that she was the one sitting here with him.

While the brothers argued over which one of them was the best looking and the smartest, Ian poured a glass of wine and handed it to her, then he filled the beer mugs all around. Gabe's shoulder brushed hers when he reached for a frosty mug, and the simple contact made her pulse skip.

The Sinclair brothers might all be good-looking, she thought, but there was only one who turned her mind to mush and her insides to gelatin. Even now, with his shoulder pressed to her shoulder, his thigh a whisper away from her thigh, she felt the burn. The rising, steady heat in her blood.

She inched away from him, reached for her wine and sipped. Anything to keep her mind off Gabe and the proximity of his body to hers.

The next number on the jukebox was Shania Twain singing about how her man better walk the line. The tune brought cheers and whistles from the women in the room and boos from the men. Reese's tavern was obviously popular with the townspeople. There were all age groups here: families, couples, singles. Everyone just out having a good time. Everyone seemed to know everyone else. And though it was different from the restaurants in Los Angeles and Beverly Hills, it felt strangely comfortable to her.

Smiling, Melanie turned her attention to her son, watched as he took Cara's hand and hurried back to the table, his face flushed with excitement.

"Did you see me, Mommy?" he asked, his eyes

wide. "I touched him. Cara said I could, and I looked inside his head, too, only it was empty."

"Hey, just like Lucian," Reese quipped, which started a volley of insults between the two brothers.

Melanie's mind spun as everyone else, including Cara, jumped in to add their own opinions on what was inside Lucian's head. Lucian was less than appreciative, and he gave back as good as he got.

Melanie had never seen anything like the Sinclair family. She had been an only child, and meals, whether they were in a restaurant or at home, were always reserved and quiet. Phillip hadn't liked conversation at the table, either, unless it was business. All this chatter and ruckus were foreign to her, and to Kevin, too. His eyes were wide, and his little head went back and forth like a Ping-Pong ball, trying to absorb every word. It was obvious he was as captivated by the Sinclairs as she was.

She glanced at the man who captivated her the most, and noticed that Gabe's attention had been diverted to the jukebox, where the redhead was now standing. Melanie saw the woman wiggle her fingers at him, then give him a knowing smile as she dropped a coin in the jukebox and push a button.

A slow song filled the tavern, and Melanie immediately recognized it as the Righteous Brothers' *Unchained Melody*. She felt Gabe stiffen beside her, then he glanced quickly away from the woman. No question there was a history here, Melanie realized and hated the stab of jealousy that shot through her. She had no business to feel anything, or think anything at all about Gabe and the redhead.

"Darn, if you were going to pick on Lucian, you should have waited for me and Abby."

The sound of the newcomer's voice jolted Melanie back to the table, and she watched as a man scooted in beside Cara, bumping her over with his hip, then pulled a pretty blonde in beside him.

Smiling, he stuck his hand out to Melanie. "I'm Callan, and this is Abby."

He was every bit as tall and handsome as the other Sinclairs, Melanie noted, and his wife was delicate, with brilliant green eyes and porcelain smooth skin. Based on the possessive touch of Callan's arm around his wife, and the look in their eyes as they glanced at each other, they were also very much in love.

The banter continued around the table, until Gabe raised his voice over everyone else and told them to be quiet.

Lucian, who'd been in the middle of a suggestion to Reese as to what he could do with his opinions, clamped his mouth shut when he remembered there was a child present.

"Melanie has good news," Gabe announced.

When everyone looked at her, Melanie felt her heart start to pound. She hardly wanted to be the center of attention.

She swallowed, glanced nervously around the table. "Well, it's a little soon to know for sure," she said hesitantly, "but it's a strong possibility that at least a few items in the house are worth a considerable amount of money."

There was a stunned silence at the table, though the conversation in the tavern was still thunderous. Melanie glanced at the jukebox again, and her pulse jumped as she realized that the redhead was making her way toward them, her gaze firmly locked on Gabe.

"Are you telling us that there's more than just garage sale junk in Mildred Witherspoon's house?" Cara asked.

Melanie forced her attention back to the table. "I've only gone through the living room and part of the dining room, but it appears that way. The Tiffany lamp in the living room alone is probably worth about fifty thousand dollars."

Cara choked, then reached for a glass of water and took a swig.

The redhead grew closer, and Melanie felt her stomach knot.

"So what now?" Abby asked when everyone else seemed too stunned to speak.

"What?" Melanie looked at Abby. "Oh, well, an auction would be best. A date will have to be set, invitations sent to the best dealers, an auctioneer hired."

"Oh, Melanie, this is so amazing." Cara reached across the table and touched her hand. "What would we do without you? Just tell us how we can help."

How they could *help?* Melanie felt a rush of panic. "But I can't...I didn't mean—"

"Hello, Gabe. Long time no see."

The redhead stood beside Gabe, one hand on her curvy hip as she smiled down at him.

"Hi, Sheila." He smiled back, and Melanie felt him shift uncomfortably on the seat beside her. "How's it going?"

"All right. How goes it with you?"

"Hey, Sheila." Reese grinned at the woman. "I heard your daddy bought you a new Porsche."

She grinned back. "He sure did. Goes real fast,

too.'' Sheila turned her attention back to Gabe. ''Wanna go for a ride?''

Melanie figured that the car wasn't the only thing that went fast, and the ride she was talking about probably had nothing to do with cars.

''Some other time,'' Gabe said stiffly. ''Ah, this is Melanie and her son, Kevin.''

Melanie forced a smile when Sheila's gaze shifted momentarily to her. The redhead nodded briefly, then looked back at Gabe. ''Can I talk to you a minute?''

''Sure.'' He looked at her expectantly.

The woman pressed her lips tightly together. ''Alone?''

''Oh, right.''

Melanie felt Gabe's fingertips brush over her thigh before he slid out of the booth. She was certain it was accidental, but nonetheless, she still felt a shiver all the way down to the tips of her toes. She watched him follow the pretty woman outside, realized that she was staring at the two, then quickly snapped her attention back to the table.

What had they been talking about? Oh, yes, the auction.

''Cara,'' Melanie said awkwardly. ''I won't be able to work the auction. I'll be leaving in a few days, and you'll need at least two weeks minimum to set everything up.''

''Well, I guess we'll just have to do what we can while you're here, then, won't we?'' Cara picked up her glass of wine and lifted it. ''And now I propose a toast. To a successful auction.''

Everyone else at the table lifted their drinks, as well. Even Kevin joined in by raising his soda, though he had no idea what he was doing. In spite of herself,

Melanie felt a thrill rush through her veins as they clinked glasses all around.

Her gaze drifted once again to the door that Gabe had just walked through with the redhead. While everyone at the table talked excitedly about the auction, she smiled and sipped her wine, tried unsuccessfully to stop her mind from wandering to thoughts of Gabe.

And suddenly she knew that her fear of staying in Bloomfield County was more than her worry that Vincent Drake would find her. Much more.

For the next three days, Gabe worked outside with the painters. Not because they needed his help. They were a good crew, more than capable of painting the house without his supervision. If anything, he was probably in their way.

Lord knew that he had more than enough work in the big house to keep him busy for another month, but with Melanie puttering around in all the rooms, the house suddenly felt small. Everywhere he turned, it seemed that she was there. He couldn't concentrate, couldn't think. He'd hear her muttering to herself as she examined some new piece of furniture, or hear her gasp as she'd open a drawer and discover some new treasure, and he'd want to go see what she'd found, he'd want to see that look of profound pleasure in her eyes.

He couldn't help but wonder what it would be like to know that he'd put that look there, not some old desk or painting. He wanted to see that flush of pleasure on her face as he moved over her, covered her body with his and filled her. He wanted to hear her moan, to feel her hands on his skin as she cried out his name.

Now, as he stood on the roof sanding an upstairs window frame, he could hear her singing softly in the bedroom next to where he was working. The window was open and he glanced over, saw the ends of the white lace curtains ripple in the warm breeze blowing through the house.

The song was familiar, a Bonnie Raitt tune about people talking. Melanie had a nice voice, he thought. Smooth and mellow. Smiling, his hand stilled as he listened.

Since that night at the tavern, it seemed to him that she'd carefully kept her distance from him. They had fallen into the routine of her cooking breakfast for him, but most of the conversation was between Kevin and him, and afterward, she'd busy herself with cleaning up, refusing to let him help, then disappear into another room. She'd offered to make him dinner, as well, but by the end of the day he was too keyed up to sit casually through a meal with her. Too frustrated.

The tension was always there between them. It hung in the air, heavy and thick, and at times it felt like a fist closing around him. She felt it, too, he was certain of that. Ever since the night of the storm, when he'd kissed her—and she'd kissed him back—there'd been an unmistakable understanding between them: He wanted her, and she wanted him, too.

All the more reason to keep his distance from her. He'd made a promise, dammit, and he'd keep it, but that didn't mean he had to like it.

But the frustration he felt wasn't just physical, he knew. She'd made it clear she would be leaving any day now. He still didn't know who she was running from, or what, and the thought of her and Kevin in any kind of danger was twisting his insides into knots. He'd hoped by now she'd trust him enough to confide in him, even a little, but she hadn't, and it was driving him crazy.

He edged his way closer to the open window of the bedroom she was in and leaned against the frame, watching her. She stood in front of a dresser bureau with her back to him, sorting through some things in a drawer. The snug fit of her jeans offered him an enticing view of her very nicely rounded rear end, and when she turned slightly, he couldn't help but notice the curve of her breasts under the plum-colored T-shirt she wore.

His palms itched just looking at her.

He knew that Kevin was taking his afternoon nap in the bedroom next door, and that nothing short of a bomb could wake the boy up. In the past three days, even with all the pounding and sanding and the spray gun motor running, Kevin hadn't stirred once during his naps. When it was time to sleep, the kid slept.

Unlike himself, Gabe thought irritably. He hadn't slept one decent night since he'd met Melanie. Every morning his sheets were tangled, damp with his sweat over the erotic, explicit dreams he'd have about her. Dreams that left him raw and aching. Not to mention downright cranky.

She bent over, opened a bottom drawer on the dresser, and his throat turned to dust at the view. She started to move her hips to the tune of her song. With a mind of its own, his body responded. His heart slammed in his chest, blood drained from the upper regions directly to the lower regions.

Oh, dear Lord. Sweat poured from his forehead.

Dammit, he was no better than some sleazy Peeping Tom, he thought, and started to back away.

That's when she shrieked.

Not a loud shriek, but enough to startle him. He lost his footing on the steep, gabled roof and started to slip. Rather than go down, he lurched his body forward and tumbled through the open window, fell flat on his face with a *thwack* on the floor.

Eyes wide, Melanie whirled and shrieked again.

Good Lord, he thought, trying to ignore the wave of pain radiating up from his jaw to the top of his head. The way he was going, he would be in a body cast any day now.

"Gabe!" Melanie rushed across the room and knelt beside him. "Gabe, are you all right?"

With a groan, he pushed himself over onto his back and stared up at the brass ceiling fan, watching the blades spin round and round. Sort of like his head.

"Fine. I'm fine." He moved his jaw back and forth, decided it wasn't broken. The only thing he'd really hurt was his pride, but, hey, that was no little thing.

When he started to push himself up on his elbows, she laid her hands on his chest and eased him back down.

"Stay still a minute," she said gently. Worry furrowed her brow. "What happened?"

"I was sanding the window frames on the upstairs bedrooms." He hardly thought it best to tell her he'd been snooping on her. "When I heard you yell, I just...slipped."

"But I didn't yell until after you—oh! Oh, yes, I guess I did." Her eyes widened as she remembered. "Oh, Gabe, you have to see this. It's so wonderful!"

She rushed back over to the dresser, and he'd barely had time to sit before she was back, kneeling beside him, holding a small white box in her hands.

"This is just one of several boxes I found today. They're Chinese, probably eighteenth century. Hand-carved ivory. From an inscription on one of the boxes, it seems that they were a gift to Mildred's grandfather, who was a sea merchant." She flipped open the lid. "Mildred kept her jewelry inside."

She pulled a cameo brooch out of the box and laid it gently in the palm of her hand. "The initials on this piece, *E.W.*, match her grandmother's, Eleanor Witherspoon. I found a family tree in Mildred's Bible."

Her voice had that same breathless quality as when she'd discovered that lamp and desk the other day. Gabe watched her fingertips caress the cameo, and the tightness he'd felt in the southern regions of his body before he'd stumbled into the bedroom returned with an intensity that had him clenching his teeth.

"There's a gold wedding band in here also, dated 1820," she went on, oblivious to the direction his mind had taken, "plus a beautiful ruby-and-diamond ring and a spectacular amethyst necklace, Victorian design. Jewelry isn't my specialty, but Simon will know. He's the best. Oh, Gabe, I can't wait to tell Cara. It's just too good to be true!"

She'd laid one hand on his arm and leaned toward him. He was trying to pay attention to what she was saying, honestly he was. But she was just so damn beautiful all fired up like this, her cheeks flushed, her eyes bright with excitement. He couldn't take his eyes off her mouth, and the sweet scent of her drifted over him like a silken net.

It was all he could do not to drag her into his arms, to roll her soft body under his and taste that incredible mouth of hers, to skim his hands down every luscious curve.

He glanced down at her hand clutching his forearm, then said tightly, "Melanie, unless you want me to break the promise I made you, you might not want to touch me right now."

She went still, then looked at her hand, realized that she was holding on to his arm. Surprised, she glanced back up at him. The look of excitement in her gray eyes turned darkly sensual, and when her gaze dropped to his mouth, his heart leaped at the sexual awareness shimmering between them.

To his profound disappointment, she dropped her hand and leaned away from him. "I—I'm sorry." Her fingers were shaking as she placed the jewelry back into the box. "I—I didn't, I mean, I wasn't—"

When she started to stand, he reached out and took hold of her hand, pulled her back down. He wanted her here, beside him, if only for another minute.

"Who's Simon?" he asked, remembering the name she'd mentioned a moment ago.

Her shoulders relaxed a bit, and she sat back on her feet. "Simon Grill, the auctioneer. He's brilliant. He not only knows antiques like nobody's business, but he also knows how to get the highest bid from the floor."

"You already hired him?"

"Cara did, and sent out the invitations, too. The dealers will be salivating over Mildred's estate." She paused, listened to the sound of the painters working with the spray gun at the back of the house. With a sigh, she turned back to him and met his gaze. "Gabe, I won't be here for the auction. I can't be."

In spite of the desire still humming in his veins, he wanted her to just talk to him, to trust him with even the tiniest bit of information about her life. He dragged in a lungful of air, then released it. "Because someone might know you?"

"Yes."

Gabe knew he should let go of Melanie's hand, but he couldn't bring himself to break even this small contact. "You could stay out of sight."

She smiled, shook her head. "You don't understand. I couldn't. I'd have to be in the middle of everything." Her smile faded as she glanced down at his hand on hers. "It would be...risky."

He told himself he should be content with just this little confidence, but he wasn't, dammit. He was more frustrated than ever. He wanted to ask more questions, bully her if he had to. Whatever it took to get her to tell him everything.

But he knew that tactic hadn't worked before and would only end up pushing her away. He didn't want to disturb this moment, possibly the first real moment that she'd let her guard down even a little bit.

They needed a neutral ground, he thought. A harmless conversation that she would be comfortable with.

"When I was in the seventh grade," he said, skimming his thumb lightly over the back of Melanie's hand, "everyone in my class had to draw the name of an elderly person in town, then do four hours' worth of chores for that person. I drew Old Lady Witherspoon."

Melanie arched one brow, waited for him to continue.

"My first day, when I showed up at her door, she looked down her glasses at me, frowned, then pointed to a rake and told me to clean up the leaves and not to bother her again until I was done. She never even asked my name." He smiled at the memory. "After four hours, I wasn't even close to being finished, but I was too damn scared of her not to keep at it. It was after dark before I bagged up the last of those damn leaves. When I finally knocked on the front door, she opened the door a crack and said, 'Are you done?' and I said, 'Yes, ma'am.'"

When he paused, Melanie leaned forward. "What did she do?"

"She said, 'Well, fine then,' and slammed the door in my face."

Melanie's eyes opened wide. "She didn't!"

"'Fraid so. I complained about it so much when I got home, my mom told me to go do something else for Miss Witherspoon, something that nobody told me to do. I admit, I sure didn't want to do anything for her after that, but I finally gave in to my mother's prodding. I went back the next day and knocked on her door, then handed her a single yellow rose I'd picked from my mom's garden."

Melanie's hand tightened in Gabe's. Outside, Gabe heard the painters laughing and the loud whir of the spray gun.

"Well," Melanie said impatiently, leaning so close he could smell the flowery scent of her shampoo. "What did she do?"

"She took it and slammed the door in my face."

Eyes wide, Melanie gasped then sat back and laughed. The sound rippled through Gabe, and he found himself laughing, as well.

"It's no wonder she never married," Gabe said. "Lord only knows what she would have done to anyone who'd have dared kiss her. Probably bury them under all that corn growing in her back field."

Melanie laughed again, then quieted as she glanced back down at their joined hands. "What about you, Gabe?" she asked quietly. "Were you ever married?"

He lifted one shoulder, shook his head. "My parents were killed in a car accident when I was twenty-four. With three younger brothers and a sister to watch out for, marriage wasn't something I was thinking about. By the time Cara graduated college, I was busy with the business."

"And now?" she asked.

"The responsibility of one family was enough for me," he said with a shrug, then grinned. "Now I'm just going to sit back and let my brothers and sister handle the family progeny."

Melanie glanced down at the cameo still in her hand, turned it around in her fingers. "I'd say that pretty redhead at the tavern the other night had other ideas."

"Sheila?" Gabe raised one brow, surprised that Melanie even remembered the woman. "Sheila's just a...friend."

She looked up, the disbelief evident in her gray eyes. "Oh?"

He shifted uncomfortably. That night at the tavern, Sheila had wanted him to stop by her house, and her innuendos that she'd wanted to do more than "talk" had not been subtle. As frustrated as he'd been feeling since he'd met Melanie, he'd almost considered the redhead's offer.

But he hadn't, of course. Going to bed with Sheila might have momentarily eased a physical discomfort, but it wouldn't have been fair to her. Gabe knew that the redhead might have been in his arms, but Melanie would have been in his mind.

"We used to date for a while," he said with a shrug. "Nothing serious."

One side of Melanie's mouth curved up, and she tilted her head. "I think Sheila might disagree with you on that. She had the look, Gabe, and it was definitely focused on you."

"Yeah? What look is that?"

She thought for a moment. "Like she's a boa constrictor and you're a big, juicy rat."

Gabe grimaced. "Gosh, thanks for the image."

She smiled at him. "It's also a look that says, 'He's mine, girls, touch him and you die.'"

He stared into Melanie's eyes, watched the soft gray turn dark and smoky, and Gabe thought if he didn't touch *her* he might die.

"All that in a look, huh?" he said lightly, though his voice was strained. "What else?"

Her smile faded, and her voice lowered. "It's a look that says you're everything she's ever hoped for, all she would ever want."

His heart slammed in his chest. "No kidding."

"There's a longing in that look," she said wistfully. "A need that is razor sharp. It could melt steel."

He didn't know about steel, but the look in Melanie's eyes right now was certainly turning his body into a raging fire. A man could only stand so much torture, he thought, gritting his teeth.

She leaned close, and her gaze dropped to his

mouth. "Gabe," she said breathlessly. "What's happening between us?"

"Hell if I know." He took her chin in his hand, ran his thumb over the smooth line of her jaw. "I made a promise to you, Melanie, but I'm only human. You've got to tell me what you want."

Something flickered in her eyes. Desire, yes, but something else. Resignation. Dammit, he wanted her willing and eager, not submissive. The woman who'd fought like a wildcat when he'd tackled her in the dark, the woman who'd slammed him in the chest with a frying pan, that woman was no quitter.

The thought was like ice water over him. Because as much as he wanted to touch her right now, to kiss her, he knew that it would only push her away from him more. She'd realize that she'd given in at a weak moment and would regret it, would hate him and probably herself, too. And there was something else here more important than the moment. Damn if he knew what it was, but he felt it in his gut.

He sighed heavily, then rolled away from her and stood, raking both hands through his hair as he faced her. "I've got to finish sanding these windows. The painters will be moving to the front of the house in a little while."

She nodded, then lifted her gaze to his. "I'm sorry," she said softly. "I wish things could be different."

"They can be. Let me help you."

"I can't."

"You mean won't."

She closed her eyes on a sigh, opened them again. "Please, Gabe, I don't want to argue with you."

Because he would have liked nothing better, Gabe

knew it was time to leave before he said something he would be sorry for. He started for the window, then stopped.

Oh what the hell, he thought. He'd already said plenty he was sorry for. What was one more thing? He turned back to her.

"Sooner or later, whatever or whoever you're running from is going to catch up to you," he said tightly. "Then you're going to have to trust somebody. I just hope like hell it won't be too late."

He climbed out the window and made his way back to the ladder crushing several of the brittle shingles under his boots. Dammit, anyway, why did everything have to be so complicated with this woman?

Well, he'd had enough. Whether she wanted it or not, whether she liked it or not, he was going to help her.

He climbed down the ladder, muttering curses with every step. Walking away from the house until he was certain he was out of earshot, he pulled his cell phone out of his shirt pocket and punched the buttons.

"It's Gabe." He looked back at the house, watched the curtains flutter in the upstairs bedroom. "I need to talk to you."

Chapter 7

"I can't believe this." Cara's fingers stroked a delicate sapphire filigree brooch, then quickly moved to a matching pair of earrings. "All this beautiful jewelry, and not once do I remember Mildred Witherspoon even wearing a ring. How could she let all these things just sit in these boxes?"

Melanie had just finished going through the last carved ivory box a few minutes ago when Cara had arrived with Ian. Rings and bracelets, earrings and necklaces, plus several brooches covered the top of the antique dresser, all laid out to be individually tagged and labeled.

Kevin suddenly tore into the room, making flying noises as he held his Caped Crusader action figure up high in one hand. He dashed around Cara, zoomed to the window, then back across the room where he made a flying leap out the door and headed into the next bedroom where he'd set up his pretend city.

Shaking her head, Melanie smiled at her son's antics, then turned back to the dresser and took in the display of exquisite antique jewelry. "This is all worth a great deal of money. It's possible that she worried about theft."

"Maybe," Cara said thoughtfully. "But Bloomfield County is hardly known for its criminal element, unless you count my brothers, of course. Oh!" With a gasp, Cara scooped up a bracelet fashioned out of interlinking silver roses and leaves. "I *adore* this!"

"Here, try it on." Melanie fastened it on Cara's wrist. "It looks wonderful on you."

"I just might have to bid on this one myself." Cara gazed longingly at the bracelet, then she sighed and took it off. "How 'bout you, Mel? Which piece is your favorite?"

"This one." Melanie picked up the cameo brooch she had been holding earlier when she'd nearly kissed Gabe. It felt warm in her hand, and she could swear she felt her fingertips tingle. She thought of his strong, firm mouth, the masculine scent of his skin, the heat of his body so close to hers…

Her body still hummed with the need he'd aroused in her.

What a fool she'd made of herself. The other night she'd made him promise that he wouldn't kiss her again, and then today she'd practically begged him to. Maybe not in words, but in her actions. She'd actually been flirting with him, for heaven's sake. She'd just gotten so caught up in the moment, she'd forgotten everything but Gabe.

She still wasn't certain if she was relieved or disappointed that he'd backed off, but she *was* certain that it was for the best.

You're going to have to trust someone, he'd told her.

How she wanted to. There were times she was so tired of running, of being afraid. Gabe would help her, she knew he would.

Could she ask?

No. She couldn't drag him into this. The last person who'd tried to help her had ended up with a broken arm for his efforts, and Melanie wouldn't risk Gabe, or any of his family, being harmed because of her.

She knew it was time for her and Kevin to leave. Past time. Not only because she'd been in one place for too long, but because the tension between her and Gabe had become unbearable. The strain of being in the same house with him day after day, sharing breakfast and an occasional lunch, being so close, it was wearing her down. She wasn't certain she could be strong for very much longer, didn't think she could resist him and what he offered.

''Melanie?''

She glanced up, realized that Cara had been talking to her. ''What?''

Cara lifted one brow, then gave her a knowing smile. ''Thinking about Gabe?''

''Gabe?'' She had to clear her throat. ''What do you mean?''

''Every time my brother is in the same room you are, or even in the vicinity, you get a certain look in your eyes. Plus you blush or get flustered if I even say his name.'' Cara folded her arms and leaned back against the dresser. ''So come on, Mel, tell Sister Cara all about it.''

Good grief, Melanie thought, here she'd been teasing Gabe about "the look" in Sheila's eyes, and now Cara was pointing out that same look was in *her* eyes.

And she *had* been thinking about Gabe.

"There's nothing to tell." Turning her attention to the jewelry, Melanie straightened the thin gold chain of a cross necklace, then fussed with a pair of early Victorian earrings. "Gabe is busy working on the house, and I've been rushing to get everything cataloged and ready for the auction. Which reminds me, have you received any RSVP's yet?"

"The phone lines at the center were jammed today with affirmatives. I'll give you a list tomorrow. And don't try to change the subject."

Cara leaned forward and whispered, "Come on, Melanie. It's my big brother we're talking about. I figure since he stuck his nose into every tiny corner of my private life up until the day I got married, and still does whenever he gets the chance, I have a right to be nosy in return. I know he's interested in you, so are you interested right back?"

"I—well—"

"Aha, you see?" Cara cocked her head and smiled. "You're blushing. So what's up with you two?"

"There's nothing up," she said and nearly choked on the last word. Something most certainly had been "up" between them a little while ago. "We're...just friends, that's all."

Cara laughed. "I've never seen Gabe look at any woman the way he looks at you. I assure you, 'friend' is not what he's thinking."

Melanie felt as if flames of fire were dancing across her face. "Cara, I don't, it isn't—"

Oh, God. Cara was right, Melanie thought with a silent groan. She did get flustered and blush if the subject was Gabe. How pathetic. She had to get a grip on herself. Stop acting like a schoolgirl and be sensible, logical. Mature.

She drew in a slow breath and faced Cara. "I am...attracted to Gabe," she admitted, pleased with herself that her voice didn't quiver. "But I'm not looking for a relationship right now, physical or otherwise. It would be much too complicated."

"Complicated is Gabe's middle name," Cara said with a grin. "And you don't have to be looking, honey. These things find you just like a Stealth fighter. Sneak right in under the radar and wham! You're a goner. Sometime I'll tell you about Ian and me."

Something told Melanie it would be a fascinating story. One she would never hear. "Cara," she said quietly, "I'm going to finish up in the last room tonight, then I'm leaving in the morning."

"Oh, Melanie." Cara sighed. "You can't leave. Stay. Let us help you. You'd be surprised what the Sinclairs and Shawnessys can accomplish when they set their minds to something. And Gabe would die before he'd let anyone hurt someone he cared about."

Cara's words sent an icy shiver up Melanie's spine. The thought of anything happening to Gabe, to Cara or Ian, or any of the Sinclairs, terrified Melanie. If she stayed here, she had a horrible feeling that something bad would happen.

Not wanting Cara to see the tears building in her eyes, Melanie leaned forward and hugged her. "I don't know how I'll ever repay you for all you've done for me and Kevin."

"Don't be silly. If it hadn't been for you, I probably would have sold that lamp downstairs for fifty bucks.'' Cara sniffed, and her voice was raspy. ''Where will you go? How will I know that you and Kevin are all right?''

''We'll be fine,'' Melanie assured her, though she wasn't so certain herself. ''I promise I'll call you when I settle in somewhere.''

Cara sighed. ''I'll always be here for you and Kevin, no matter what. If you ever need anything, anything at all, call me or Gabe.''

''Thank you.''

They were both sniffing now. Cara pulled away, blinking back her tears. ''Okay, how about this. There's a magician coming into the center tonight to perform for the children, then cake and ice cream after his act. Why don't you and Kevin come?''

Melanie shook her head, felt the heaviness in her chest. ''I have one more room to catalog—Mildred's bedroom. I decided to save hers for last.''

''Then let Ian and me take Kevin,'' Cara said. ''He'll love the show and being with the other kids. And we'd love to spend a little more time with him before you go. We don't want him to forget us.''

The idea of letting Kevin out of her sight terrified Melanie, but she knew that Cara was right. Before their world had been turned upside down, Kevin had loved playing with the other children at his preschool. He'd been only with her for the past several weeks and other adults, and she knew he was bored. He seemed all right now, but today, after he'd woken up from his nap, he'd been unusually cranky.

She trusted Cara and Ian implicitly. If anything, he would probably be safer with them. Vincent might enjoy intimidating women and men smaller and weaker than himself, but face-to-face with a large, strong man like Ian, he would be a coward.

But Vincent hadn't found her here, she was certain of that. He would have had several opportunities to confront her when she'd been alone, and she knew he wouldn't have waited. He wasn't the patient type.

How could she say no to Cara? Kevin would love a magic show. And Melanie also knew that she'd be able to finish her work more quickly without Kevin under her feet.

She sucked in a deep breath, then nodded. "All right, but, Cara, please...well, I know that—"

"Stop worrying. We won't let him out of our sight for a second." Cara hugged her quickly. "I'll be right back. I'm going to go tell Kevin."

Her insides shaking, Melanie leaned back against the dresser. Of course he would be fine. Cara was right. She had to stop worrying.

Outside, she heard the hum of the paint sprayer. She moved to the window and saw Russell, the foreman spraying a fresh coat of blue on the downstairs level. Even with the window closed, she could smell the paint and cleaners they used. The house was going to be beautiful when they finished, and she felt another pang of regret that she wouldn't be here to see it.

She started to turn away when she noticed Gabe and Ian standing under a large oak several yards away from the house. Gabe had his back to her, and Ian, his arms folded, leaned against the tree trunk. Ian's head was bent, but even from here she could see the frown on his face.

"Mommy! I'm going to a magic show!"

Kevin ran into the room and hugged her, nearly

knocking her over in his excitement. His cheeks were flushed, his blue eyes bright with pleasure.

"I know, sweetie, isn't that wonderful?" She bent down and hugged him back, praying that she'd made the right decision.

"You're asking a lot, Gabe."

Gabe looked at his brother-in-law and nodded. "I know that, believe me, I know it. But no one has the resources you do, Ian. I need to know who this woman is, and what she's running from. You could find out."

"I left the agency when I married your sister. I'm a civilian now."

"You still have connections. You know who to ask."

Ian sighed. "Gabe, she doesn't want anyone to know about her life, doesn't want our help. What right do we have to interfere?"

Gabe thought of Melanie and Kevin, wandering from town to town, maybe not knowing where they would eat or sleep next. And worse, the thought of someone hurting her or Kevin, made his chest tighten.

"You know I wouldn't ask if it wasn't important," Gabe said evenly.

"You haven't known her that long."

Gabe shook his head. "Doesn't matter. I have to do this, with or without your help."

Ian studied Gabe for a long moment. "Does she feel the same way about you?"

"I don't know what I'm feeling, dammit. And I sure as hell don't know what she's thinking. All I know is that she plans on leaving any day now, and

I won't ever see her or Kevin again. I won't know where they are, if they're all right."

He raked both hands through his hair and started to pace. "I can't accept that, Ian. I won't. I'm not going to turn my back on this anymore."

And besides, he thought, she was leaving anyway. What did he have to lose?

"Look." Gabe stopped, put his hands on his hips. "When Cara was in trouble and you knew someone was trying to kill her, you called me and told me to watch her for you, even though you knew that she would be furious with you for interfering."

Ian pressed his lips tightly together. "That was different."

"The hell it was. Cara was stubborn and independent and wanted to do everything her way. You made a decision not to let her and you were right. Well, dammit, I'm making that same decision now with Melanie, and I know I'm right, too."

Ian dropped his head back and groaned. "You Sinclairs have got to be the most mule-headed bunch I've ever met."

"Does that mean you'll help me?"

Ian blew out a breath. "Yeah, I'll help you. But be warned, buddy. You might not like what I find."

"I'm sure I won't." Gabe glanced back at the house, watched as the two women walked out onto the front porch, then repeated quietly, "I'm sure I won't."

Melanie thought that the best word to describe Mildred Witherspoon's bedroom was somber. The quilt on her four-poster walnut bed was hand-sewn with shades of brown and green, the walls were faded gray and the old, braided oval rug a blend of dull, drab colors.

It was true that the house in general wasn't exactly what anyone would call bright and cheerful, but it almost seemed as if the old woman had intentionally robbed this particular room—her bedroom—of any life.

Melanie thought of the conversations she'd had with the elderly woman. She hadn't seemed as unpleasant as Gabe had suggested. There'd been something in the woman's voice, a loneliness, that had touched Melanie. And though it had only been on the phone, they'd had a friendship, of sorts, with Mildred always remembering to ask about Kevin. Melanie was sorry she'd never had the chance to meet the woman.

Melanie glanced at her watch. It was only six o'clock. Cara and Ian had left with Kevin maybe twenty minutes ago, and they wouldn't be back until close to ten. So long, she thought, and felt the hitch in her chest. They hadn't been away from each other for weeks now, and while she knew it was good for both of them, she still missed him. She still worried.

The house was so quiet. A sad, lonely quiet. The painters had left an hour ago, and Gabe had left shortly after that. It was silly, but she'd been disappointed when he'd said goodbye to her and Kevin and driven off. She'd almost done something extremely foolish and asked him to stay and have dinner with her, but thank goodness she'd caught herself before the words had come out. She knew that for the two of them to be alone here would be a mistake. A big mistake.

Melanie opened the door of the closet, and the scent of cedar and old leather wafted out. She stepped inside, surprised that the closet was so large, then pulled the chain for the overhead lamp. Light spilled over all the neatly hung clothes. It seemed that the lack of color extended to Mildred's wardrobe, as well, Melanie noted. Long, matronly dresses, all blacks and grays, burgundies and dark greens, filled the hangers. Shoes sat primly on the hardwood floor, hat boxes were piled on the upper shelves and cardboard boxes of all sizes completely filled one wall.

This shouldn't take long at all, Melanie thought. Maybe an hour at the most. She felt gritty from the day and decided she'd take a quick shower before she finished up in here.

And then she'd have a long night ahead of her.

Alone.

The sun had sunk below the horizon and dusk edged into darkness by the time Gabe drove back to the Witherspoon house. The air was comfortably warm, and an evening breeze carried the scent of freshly plowed earth from a neighboring farm.

Gabe stepped out of his truck, listened to the sound of the cornstalks swaying in the breeze and the music of a nearby whippoorwill. He glanced at the big oak beside the garage and could picture a tire swing on one massive limb, or a tree house, like the one he and his dad had built when he was ten.

He smiled at the memory, remembering all those great summer nights he'd slept up in the rough plywood structure with his brothers when they were all little. Or when he'd gotten older and sneaked a pack of cigarettes up there. His dad had caught him and insisted he smoke the whole pack, inhaling, of course. Gabe winced at that memory. He hadn't gotten past six cigarettes before he'd thrown up. That had been the end of smoking for him. His dad had ruled with a firm hand, but a loving one.

He missed his parents terribly, but he knew how lucky he was to have his brothers and sister. He'd never felt the need for more, had decided long ago that raising one family was enough.

So then why was he thinking about tire swings and tree houses?

With a sigh, he glanced at the house, saw that it was dark, but knew that Melanie was inside. He also knew that Kevin had gone with Cara and Ian, and that they wouldn't be back until later. Which was exactly the reason he'd left earlier. He'd told himself that he was going to the tavern tonight. It was Saturday night. There was a big game on the sports network, and Reese usually had a friendly, late-night poker game going after he closed up the tavern. If he decided to drink too much—and he just might—then he'd crash there.

He'd told himself all through his shower and then while he'd gotten dressed that he wasn't going back to the Witherspoon house tonight. What was the point? He was already twisted up like a pretzel, why subject himself to more frustration?

The Witherspoon house wasn't on the way from his apartment to the tavern, so how the hell had he ended up over here, and why had he turned down the driveway? he thought in disgust.

And why had he already parked his pickup and walked into the house?

Dammit, anyway. The woman made him crazy.

"Melanie?" he called out quietly, not wanting to startle her.

He listened for her to reply, but all he heard was quiet. He'd expected her to be in the kitchen, but realized that with Kevin gone, she probably wouldn't prepare a meal.

Maybe she'd come to the tavern with him, he thought and made his way up the stairs. Or there was the steak and seafood place just outside of town, that was a nice place, with tablecloths and candles and quiet music. But he only had on jeans and a black T-shirt, probably not the right attire for—

What the hell was he thinking?

He wasn't going to ask her anywhere, he thought with a scowl. He'd just check on her, make sure she was all right, and then he'd leave.

So where the hell was she?

"Melanie?"

He stood at the bottom of the stairs. The house was nearly dark, yet he saw no light from any of the bedrooms. Maybe she'd fallen asleep. Lord knew she worked hard enough. The woman never stopped, and she had a four-year-old to care for, as well.

He called to her again, but still no answer. A tiny knot of worry twisted in his stomach. She could be sick. Or maybe she hurt herself. Or maybe someone—

Oh, God.

He took the stairs three at a time. "Melanie!"

"I'm back here," came her muffled reply.

Relief pounded through Gabe, and he moved to the last bedroom. A sliver of light poured into the dark bedroom from the closet. He peeked in the closet and saw her sitting on the floor, her legs folded under her. She'd changed into soft gray sweatpants and a tank top, and she'd piled her hair on top of her head.

She looked up at him and frowned.

"You scared me. Why were you yelling like that?"

She was surrounded by ledgers of some kind, he noticed, and a large cardboard box beside her held several more. His heart was still pounding, but he leaned casually against the closet doorjamb. "What'cha doing?"

Her frown disappeared, and she beamed at him. "Oh, Gabe, you won't believe this. It's so amazing."

"What?" He pushed away from the doorjamb and hunkered down beside her. She smelled like soap and flowers, and he resisted the urge to lean closer and take a deep breath of her.

"Mildred's diaries." She gestured toward the cardboard box. "From the time she was fourteen up until the night she died. After I found all these, I checked her nightstand and found the most current journal in the drawer."

"Old Lady Witherspoon kept a diary?" Gabe picked up one hardbound journal book and stared at it. "What would she have to write about?"

"She wrote about everything," Melanie said breathlessly. "Her thoughts and feelings, what she did every day, Bloomfield and all the people. Do you know a man named Robert Carper?"

"Sure. He used to be the manager at Winkie's Market. He retired at least ten years ago. Why?"

"Mildred had a thing for him, that's why. She said he reminded her of Clark Gable."

Clark Gable? Well, Bob did have big ears, but any other similarity, Gabe thought, was lost on him. "That's hard to swallow. I was only a kid at the time, maybe fourteen, but I worked there one summer as a bagger. Before Mildred had her groceries delivered, she used to come in twice a week and every time she complained about something.''

''That was so she could talk to him,'' Melanie explained. ''She said he made her heart flutter.''

''Bob?'' Gabe gave a dry laugh. ''Any flutters in Old Lady Witherspoon's chest had to be a heart condition.''

Melanie rolled her eyes. ''Is it so hard to believe she had feelings?''

''Yes.'' Gabe sat down beside Melanie, felt his own heart slam in his chest when he realized she wasn't wearing a bra.

''Well, she did. She admitted it hurt her when she wasn't invited to Claire Wilson's wedding.''

Now it was Gabe's turn to roll his eyes. ''Claire and Harry Wilson just celebrated their fiftieth anniversary, for God's sake.''

Melanie sighed. ''It seems that Mildred had a long memory.''

At this moment, Gabe thought, his own memory was quite short-term. All he could think about was how close he'd come to kissing Melanie earlier, about the kiss they'd already shared. About how badly he wanted to pull her in his arms and kiss her again.

''In fact,'' Melanie went on, ''Mildred had something to say about you.''

''Me?'' Gabe dragged his mind from where it didn't belong back to the conversation. ''She said something about me?''

Melanie smiled slowly, then reached for a journal behind her and handed it to Gabe. ''Open this.''

Wary, Gabe took the journal, then opened it to the page where something had been slipped between the pages.

A dried, flattened rose.

A yellow rose.

Gabe glanced up at Melanie, saw the delight dancing in her eyes as she watched him.

"Read that page," she said softly.

He looked back at the journal, noted the date at the top of the page. Saturday, October 15, 1979.

That was twenty-one years ago, Gabe realized. Stunned, he read on.

> Little Gabriel Sinclair—well, not so little, the child must be nearly six feet tall!—knocked on my door this morning and informed me that he was here to do four hours of chores for me and asked what I would like him to do. I told him to rake the leaves and not to knock on my door and bother me until every last leaf was raked. Oh, my, the look of fear in his eyes did make me chuckle when I closed the door. What a pleasure it was for me to watch him work that day. How it reminded me of when I was a child and I would run and laugh and fall into the mountains of leaves I would sweep up. But that was before Papa died and Mama forbid any laughter in the house. I made a glass of lemonade and sat by the window, watching Gabriel the whole day. I know he was too afraid of me not to finish and though I wanted to tell him to stop, to come and sit and have a glass of lemonade with me, I was too afraid. What if he laughed at me, told all his friends what a crazy old lady I am. I know that's what they all say, anyway.

The next entry was Sunday, October 16.

Little Gabriel knocked on my door again today. A rose! He brought me a beautiful yellow rose. The most beautiful rose in the world, I'm sure. For a very long moment, I was too stunned to speak, then all I could manage to do was slam the door before he saw the tears in my eyes. I am such a silly old fool, but never in my entire life has anyone ever given me a flower of any kind. He is a handsome one, Gabriel. I pray he will not break hearts, the way mine was broken so very long ago.

Dazed, Gabe looked up at Melanie. Her eyes were bright with moisture. "She kept the rose I gave her?"

Melanie nodded. "I skimmed most of the journals and she mentioned you several times. Maybe a comment about how tall you'd grown, or how handsome. How brave you were at your parents' funeral, and how well you took care of your brothers and sister. She was quite fond of you."

"Because I gave her a rose?" he asked incredulously. "I can't believe she even remembered."

"She more than remembered." Melanie leaned close, her eyes wide. "Gabe, she left her house to the Shawnessy Foundation because of you, because of that rose."

"What?" He was glad he was sitting because he was certain she would have knocked him over on that comment. "What are you talking about?"

"She was familiar with the Killian Shawnessy Foundation because of the fund-raising you and your brothers have done here in Bloomfield County. She mentioned an annual Chili Bake-Off just three months ago, which I understand your sister always wins,"

Melanie added with a smile. "Mildred didn't attend, but she read in the paper that Sinclair Construction sponsored the event and all the proceeds went to the center. That was enough for her. She decided then to call her attorney and have him make the foundation her sole beneficiary."

Gabe stared at the rose. It was the palest yellow, the leaves had long crumbled and the stem had turned brown. But this single rose had been something extremely important in Mildred's life.

And now, in his life, too.

Because he never would have come to this house after Mildred had died, wouldn't have met Melanie and Kevin, wouldn't be sitting here right now with a woman he wanted more than any woman he'd ever met in his entire life.

He sucked in a breath, looked at Melanie and actually managed to speak. "She said her heart had been broken. Did she say who the man was?"

"I found her earlier journals," Melanie said. "She wrote about her love for a man named William McDaniels. He was a drifter, doing odd jobs around town. Her mother had hired him to make some repairs around the house. Mildred fell instantly and madly in love, and she thought that William loved her, as well. They were going to run off and be married, Mildred thought, even though her mother disapproved. When William's wife and two children showed up in town looking for him, Mildred was devastated. She never got over it, never really trusted anyone after that. She never told anyone."

"Who would have thought?" Gabe shook his head. "Old Lady Witherspoon was once young and in love."

''Everyone falls in love sometime,'' Melanie said quietly as she gently closed the book and replaced it in the box. ''And everyone has their heart broken, too. Some people get over it and some don't.''

He realized she wasn't talking about Mildred, but herself. He reached out and cupped her chin in his hand, lifted her face to his. ''Who broke your heart, Melanie?'' he asked.

The wistful look in her eyes made his chest tighten. ''I was young and in love, too, and when I married, I truly believed it was forever. My husband didn't.''

Dread welled up in Gabe's chest. Was that why she kept her distance, he wondered. Why she wouldn't let him close? Because she still loved her husband?

''Do you still love him?'' he asked tightly.

''No.'' She leaned into his hand, and he felt her warm breath on his wrist. ''But I don't want to talk about my late husband. Not now.''

The texture of her smooth, soft skin fascinated him, aroused him. He skimmed the curve of her jaw with his fingertips. ''You don't?''

''No.'' She pressed her mouth to the palm of his hand, and he sucked in a breath at the touch of her soft lips. ''Gabe?''

''What?'' He had to struggle to get the single word out.

''Make love to me.''

Chapter 8

Gabe went very still. It almost seemed to Melanie that the entire world had stilled. A quiet calm settled over her, and for the first time since she'd met Gabe, for the first time in her life, she felt completely at ease, confident of who she was and what she wanted.

She wanted him. And if it could only be for this one night, then she would accept that.

"Gabe." She said his name again, a whisper, then covered his hand with hers. "I want you to make love to me."

She saw the surprise in his deep green eyes, the hesitation. She understood it. After all, she'd pushed him away at every turn, even made him promise to keep his distance. Why would she expect him to believe her now that she was sincere?

But from the beginning, this need had been here between them. She'd tried to deny it, to refuse it, but she couldn't any longer. She might as well deny her next breath.

How strange to think that it was Mildred herself who'd tipped the scales, Melanie thought. That a story about yellow roses and a lost love would make her see what was really in her heart? She wanted—needed—Gabe to know how important he was to her, how important he would always be to her.

"Melanie." His hand tightened under hers, tension radiated from his body. "You have to be sure."

"I'm sure." She turned her head and pressed her mouth to his hand. It was large and callused, the texture rough against her lips. She'd watched those hands hold a hammer, sand wood, mix cement. Throw a baseball to her son.

And now she wanted them on her.

When she took his hand and brought it to her breast, she heard his muffled groan.

Lifting her gaze to his, she saw the raw desire in his eyes. The intensity took her breath away. When he glanced down to where their hands were joined over her breast, she saw that desire darken. Heat flooded her body, made her limbs feel soft and liquid, her skin tight and tingly.

"Melanie." His voice was ragged, hoarse. "As badly as I want you, I don't want you to regret this."

She shook her head slowly, held his dark gaze. "No regrets."

His gaze narrowed, dropped to her mouth. "I haven't slept since I met you. You've been driving me crazy."

"I haven't even started yet," she said, shocked by her own brazen manner, then ever-so-slightly moved her hardened nipple against his hand.

On a groan, he reached for her, wrapping his arms around her and dragging her against his rock-hard chest. His mouth swooped down and covered hers, a hard, demanding kiss that made her senses reel. She wrapped her arms around his neck, met the deep thrust of his tongue with her own. He tasted like minty toothpaste, his aftershave smelled spicy and masculine. She felt her blood rush through her veins, hot and wild, building in pressure.

He kissed her over and over, as if he couldn't get enough of her. A long, hot, never-ending kiss that left her gasping. No one had ever kissed her like this, she thought dimly. So completely, so thoroughly, so desperately. She'd been a virgin when she'd married Phillip, and sex between them had always been straightforward, an activity that a husband and wife engaged in, and though she'd never thought it unpleasant, she'd never experienced anything even close to what she was feeling at this moment with Gabe. She'd never even imagined this kind of passion.

The thought exhilarated her as much as it frightened her. There would never be anyone like Gabe again, she was certain of that. There couldn't be.

But there was no going back now; she wouldn't even if she could. Every moment in her life had brought her here, to Gabe. Even if it was only for one night, this was where she belonged, with Gabe. She knew it in her heart and her soul.

She felt the tension and need shimmer from Gabe's body into hers, knew that he needed her every bit as much as she needed him.

His name shuddered out from her lips.

The urgency increased, and in one quick movement, his hot mouth rushed over her jaw, down her neck. She shivered, let her head fall backward, offering herself to him, wanting his mouth and hands on her everywhere all at once.

"I wasn't going to come here tonight," he said roughly, then gently sank his teeth into the sensitive flesh under her earlobe. "I couldn't stand being so close to you and not touching you. I knew I would have to break my promise to you."

"Oh, Gabe." She sighed, ran her fingers through his thick hair while he busied his lips with the rapidly beating pulse at the base of her throat. "I was a fool to think I could stop this from happening. We're not children, we both knew what we wanted from the beginning. But you frightened me."

He stilled, then lifted his head. His eyes glinted darkly with passion; confusion furrowed his brow. "I frightened you?"

"No one's ever looked at me like you did, like you're looking at me right now, with such fierce need. You overwhelmed me, but excited me at the same time. Sometimes I'd watch you working, and I'd want you so badly it was all I could do to keep myself from throwing you to the ground and jumping you."

Surprise lit the darkness in his eyes. He shook his head slowly, chuckled when he touched her cheek with his fingertips. "Sweetheart, you are one great big mystery to me."

She reached for him, drew his mouth back to hers. "No more talk," she whispered. "Touch me."

Gabe had thought that he would never hear those words from her, and her soft plea stretched the already thin thread of his control. She'd said they weren't children, but his need for her raged inside him so fiercely he felt like a randy teenager in the back seat of his father's Buick.

Though it was the last thing he wanted to do, he slowed himself down, struggled to contain the urge to take her fast and hard. With her hands roaming over his shoulders and her lips nibbling on his, he was certain that taking it slow was going to be the hardest thing he'd ever done in his life.

When she leaned forward and pressed her soft breasts against him, when he felt the hard buds of her nipples burn into his chest, he thought that slow just might kill him.

He eased her back onto a neatly folded, cream-colored knitted afghan lying on the floor of the closet. Her lips were swollen and wet from his kisses, her cheeks flushed. Opening her eyes, she watched him through a glaze of passion.

His throat felt dry; blood pumped through his body, pooled below his waist. This was what he'd dreamed of night after night, but the reality was so much more than the fantasy. He reached for the soft cotton edge of her tank top, slowly edged his hands underneath. Her stomach was flat and firm, her skin warm and smooth, the texture of silk. Her eyes narrowed when he spread his fingers wide, covering her belly, and when he slid his hands and fabric upward, she bit her bottom lip and closed her eyes again.

He paused just below the underside of her full, round breasts, skimmed the soft flesh there with his knuckles. She whimpered softly, squirmed.

"Touch me," she breathed. "Please."

Barely holding onto his control, he pushed the fabric up out of his way, felt his heart jump into his throat as he stared at her. God, but she was beautiful. So perfect.

And for the moment, she was his. Completely his.

He leaned down, kissed the soft, ultrasensitive skin around one rosy nipple, then took the beaded tip into his mouth. She arched upward, dug her fingers into his scalp as she gasped. He lavished his attention on that sweet spot, used his tongue and lips to pleasure her. Her fingernails raked over his head and down his back, igniting every nerve along their path.

"Take this off," she said roughly, tugging at his T-shirt. "I need to touch you."

He rose to his knees, reached for his shirt. She surged upward. "Let me."

Her hands slid underneath the black cotton and pushed the fabric up. He yanked the shirt off, then sucked in a breath at the touch of her soft fingers on his chest. When she pressed her lips to his skin, as he had done to her, a thunderbolt of pleasure shot through his body. She nuzzled him with her lips and tongue while her fingers slid through the sprinkling of dark hair on his chest. When her hands moved downward, over his belly to his belt buckle, he moaned.

Maybe slow wasn't such a good idea after all.

They were both on their knees, torso to torso, hot bare skin to hot bare skin. He struggled to breathe while she unhooked the buckle of his belt, and when she looked up at him, he gripped her shoulders and once again caught her mouth with his. Her tongue met his, stroke for stroke, and he felt a sudden fury to possess this woman body and soul. The thought staggered him, but when her busy hands unsnapped his jeans and reached for the zipper, he was way beyond thought.

Melanie's breath caught at the fierce grip Gabe had on her shoulders. She felt his need shudder from his body into hers and when she reached blindly for the zipper on his jeans, his assault on her mouth bordered on violent. She felt raw and exposed, every nerve turned inside out as she met his need with her own. She'd never considered herself short, but kneeling in front of Gabe, nearly naked, with his tall, muscular body dwarfing her, she suddenly felt small and vulnerable.

And yet, strangely, knowing that he wanted her with such intensity also made her feel powerful, as well. His kiss was hungry, consuming, and tiny shock waves of pleasure rippled through her as he tasted her again and again.

She slowly lowered the zipper on his jeans, and the feel of his arousal against her hand excited her. With trembling hands, she slipped her fingers under the band of his jeans and briefs and tugged them down.

At the same time, Gabe's hands slid down her arms, slipped under the elastic waistband of her sweats and eased the garment down.

His work-roughened hands slid over the curve of her rear end and cupped her. She drew in a breath at the exquisite feel of his callused palms on her skin, and when he pulled her against him and she felt the hard, velvet-steel of his erection against her belly, she gasped.

Her arms snaked around his neck and she rose against him, her body hot and aching for him. She wanted, *needed* him inside her.

But they were still wearing too many clothes, she

realized, and pulled away again, dragging her mouth down his chest while she eased his jeans lower still. She murmured a protest when they would go no farther, and he rolled away from her to yank off his boots and the rest of his clothes. When he turned back to her, naked, with a fierce, primal glint in his eyes, her heart slammed in her chest.

He reached for her, tugged her underneath him, then rose over her while he slipped her sweatpants and underwear down her legs and tossed them aside.

He was so magnificent, his chest broad, his shoulders muscled, and she knew in her heart that she would never be the same after this night. She knew at some instinctive, basic level, that their joining would profoundly alter her existence.

The muscles in his powerful arms stood out like thick cords as he lowered his body to hers. He watched her, his face a sculpture of hard, sharp angles, and she felt as if he could see inside her, that he knew her every thought, every secret. The very idea that he might have that power frightened her for a moment, but her need for him pushed the thought aside.

And as he slid into her, all she could do was feel.

The ache that had been pulsing through her veins turned into a living thing. She rose to meet him, bringing him deeper inside of her. Her arms wound around his neck, her fingers dug into his scalp, then moved restlessly over his powerful back. She felt his strong muscles bunch and ripple under her hands as he moved. Pleasure spiraled through her like a hot wind, whirled faster and faster. Higher. Hotter.

Gasping, she called out his name, moved with him stroke for stroke. His skin was damp under hers, and the male scent of him invaded her senses, sending her higher still. She held on, called out his name on a sob when her release came in an explosion of color and sound. The waves were still moving through her when, on a low, deep groan, he buried his face in her neck and shuddered against her.

Peace settled over her as she wrapped her arms around his neck and sighed. She felt her smile touch not only her lips, but her heart, as well.

At thirty-five, Gabe had never been a saint, nor had he pretended to be. He thought it was natural for two people who were attracted to each other to end up in bed, and whenever he had been in a relationship, he'd always believed that it should be exclusive. He'd genuinely cared for every woman who had been in his life and was still friends with most of them.

But now, lying here on this hardwood floor, in Mildred Witherspoon's closet, holding Melanie in his arms, he couldn't imagine ever being "friends."

She'd quite literally knocked his socks off.

He tightened his hold on her and pulled her closer. With a sigh, she snuggled against him, burying her face into his chest. He pressed his mouth to her temple, breathed in the fresh scent of her hair into his lungs. Neither one of them had spoken since they'd made love, and the quiet settled over them like a warm blanket.

Her body fit perfectly to his, and he tucked her closer still. "You all right?" he asked carefully.

"Hmm."

He took that as a yes. "This floor must be killing you."

"Uh-uh."

Making love had obviously exhausted her, but Gabe felt energized, as if he could leap tall buildings in a single bound. He also felt as if he could eat the proverbial horse. "You hungry?"

"Starving," she muttered weakly.

"We could go into town, to the tavern or somewhere else, if you like." He didn't want to, didn't want to leave here and share this precious time with anyone else. But he thought he should ask. "We'd be back before Kevin gets home."

Her fingers moved softly back and forth on his chest and her touch sent an arrow of heat straight down. "I don't want to go anywhere."

Relief poured through him. He tightened his hold on her, kissed her cheek. She turned her head and met his lips with her own. It was a soft kiss, tender.

"Thank you," she murmured against his mouth.

Thank you? She'd just given him the single most moving experience of his life, and she was thanking *him?* He chuckled softly. Good Lord, but this woman never ceased to amaze him.

"Anytime," he teased.

She lifted her head. "I mean it, Gabe," she whispered. "I can't remember when I ever felt so wonderfully alive."

Her words, and the intensity in her dove-gray eyes made his throat turn to dust. The desire that had been sated only minutes before rose again, as hot and wild as ever.

He wouldn't let this woman go, he thought desperately. He couldn't. Surely she'd change her mind and stay. How could she possibly leave now, after this?

Almost savagely, he covered her mouth with his,

rolled her underneath him. She rose up and met him, slid her arms around his shoulders and kissed him back with an urgency that made the blood roar in his ears.

He didn't mean to be rough, but he simply lost control. He entered her fast and hard and she gasped, arching upward as she took him into the tight, warm sheath of her body. Breathing ragged, muscles strained, he filled her, and when he laced his fingers with hers and lifted her slender arms over her head, pinning her beneath him, she sucked a sharp breath through her teeth and shivered.

"Gabe," she cried out on a sob. "Now, please, *now.*"

He moved, and she wrapped her long, silky legs around him, drawing him deeper inside her.

"Open your eyes," he said hoarsely, still holding her arms. "Look at me."

Her heavy lids fluttered open, and her smoke-colored eyes were glazed with desire. She met his gaze, held it, and he felt as if he'd fallen into a dark, swirling well of intense pleasure.

He drove himself into her, and she met him with every thrust. She bit her lip, rolled her hips violently, then shuddered into him, and he followed, his jaw clenched, his body convulsing. Completion ripped through him, and he groaned deeply, the sound primal.

When he could breathe again, when he could move, he gathered her in his arms and held her close.

It was eight forty-five before they made it down to the kitchen. Gabe kissed her long and hard by the kitchen sink, then suggested sandwiches while he nibbled on her neck.

Limp from his kiss, she sucked in a breath, struggled to gain control. "We'll never eat if you keep doing that."

"Okay." He caught her earlobe between his teeth and nipped.

Her laugh was breathless as she pushed him away. "Food, Sinclair. I need sustenance. Lunch meat's in the refrigerator door."

To her relief, and disappointment, he sighed, then moved away.

"Got any lettuce in here?"

Melanie glanced over her shoulder and looked at Gabe. He was barefoot, like herself, his hair mussed, like hers, and he was busy rooting around in the back of the small refrigerator. The view he offered of snug jeans stretched tight over his butt made her heart trip. Gabriel Sinclair was the most perfect specimen of male that she'd ever laid eyes on.

And most certainly that she'd ever laid her hands on, she thought with a smile.

"It's in the bottom drawer," she answered, and reached for the loaf of bread on the counter. "There's a tomato in there, too, if you want."

A package of ham in one hand and sliced cheese in the other, he slammed the refrigerator door shut with his hip and moved beside her.

"That will take too long," he murmured from behind her. He dropped the packages on the counter, circled her waist with his arms, bent to press his mouth to the back of her neck. "How much time do we have left before Kevin gets home?"

"Cara said—" her breath caught when Gabe's

warm, wet tongue slid over her bare skin "—they'd be back around ten."

A shiver raced from the spot where his lips touched her straight down to her toes. She fumbled with the tie on the bread.

He'd pinned her between the counter and his hard body, and she gave up on the bread and leaned back against him. His mouth roamed over her shoulders, pausing to nibble here and there, and his hands slid upward under her tank top to cup her breasts.

How could she want him again so soon? she wondered. This was so new to her, so incredible. One hand slid downward, under the waistband of her sweats.

So thrilling.

He cupped her, brought her rear end flush with his body while he nibbled on her neck, then murmured exciting, erotic things in her ear. Gasping, she pressed against him, wanting him to do all those things he whispered and more.

His hand slid under her panties, and he slipped one finger into her, stroking her while his teeth worked on her ear. She gripped the counter, thought her knees might give out, she felt so weak.

Fire raced through her blood as he stroked her, and the ache tightened, a pain-pleasure that centered between her legs and built to an urgency that demanded release. His hold tightened on her when she cried out and jerked backward. She shattered against him, fell bonelessly back when the shudders finally subsided.

"Gabe," she whispered. "What are you doing to me?"

"Making love to you, sweetheart." He turned her

in his arms, smiled down at her as he kissed her nose. "I believe you asked me to."

She had, she remembered, and felt her cheeks warm. "You've done more than make love to me," she said softly. "Much more."

"Tell me, Melanie." His gaze turned dark and insistent. "Tell me what I've done."

He'd gotten in where she'd sworn no man would again. Into her heart. Somehow, she'd fallen in love with this man, and she could bring nothing but hurt and misery to him. But she couldn't tell him that. He wouldn't understand, he couldn't understand.

"You've been a friend," she said simply. "A wonderful friend when I needed one."

"Friend?" He frowned at her. "I'm not liking the sound of this."

"Gabe." She took his face in her hands. "I wanted to tell you earlier, really I did." She drew in a slow breath. "I'm leaving tomorrow."

His frown turned to a scowl. "Like hell you are."

She sighed. "There's no place for you and me, for any kind of a relationship, to go. It will be easier for both of us when I'm gone."

"Easy?" He snatched her hands away, took a step back. "Maybe you think running away is easy, but I call it chicken. You're a big girl, Melanie. When are you going to learn to face your problems?"

She'd suspected he wouldn't take this well, but she hadn't expected such fierce anger. She swallowed hard, struggled to steady herself. But of course he was angry. He had every right to be.

"You can't understand—"

"You don't know jack about me if you believe that." He grabbed her shoulders, and she felt his fury in the bite of his fingers. "Try me, dammit. I deserve something here, other than this 'it was great, see you around' number you keep singing."

"Take your hands off me."

"Not until you talk to me."

"I won't be bullied, Gabe."

His fingers dug deeper into her arms. "Nothing else has worked with you, goddammit. Why the hell can't you see I want to help you? Why the hell can't you trust me just once?"

She stared at him in shock. They'd just made love, didn't he have any idea what that meant to her? Of course she trusted him. How could he be such an idiot?

Something snapped in her. All these weeks of running, the months of living in her mother-in-law's house and being under her control, the physical threats and intimidation from Vincent, the fact that he was hunting for her right now, and would bring her back at any cost. It all swirled in her mind like a fiery tornado.

Dammit! She didn't deserve this! Any of this.

Blind with rage, she pushed away from him.

"You're no better than they are," she said in a low, fierce voice. "I refused to give in to them, and I won't give in to you. Do you understand? It's *my* life. Mine and Kevin's."

"Who?" he asked quietly, carefully keeping his distance. "Tell me who they are."

"No." She swallowed the thickness in her throat, refusing to cry. She *wouldn't* cry. "You can't help. You think you can, but you can't. This isn't just about me, Gabe, don't you understand that? This is about my son, and there's nothing on this earth that will make me take risks where he's concerned.''

She backed up against the counter, the same counter where he'd loved her only minutes ago. It was all she could do not to sink on her knees in front of him, to let him take her in the comfort of his arms and make this nightmare go away.

But she couldn't. And he couldn't.

''Kevin and I are leaving in the morning,'' she said quietly, somehow managing to make her voice even and strong. ''I hope you'll come and say goodbye to both of us.''

A muscle twitched in his temple; his face was a tight mask of controlled anger. ''I'll be here.''

She lowered her voice, let her eyes plead with him. ''Please, Gabe, I don't want our last words to be harsh, not after tonight.''

''You can't just expect—''

''Melanie?'' Cara's voice called out from the other room. ''We're back.''

So soon? Melanie felt the blood drain from her face. She didn't want Cara and Ian, and especially Kevin, to see her and Gabe like this. ''Gabe, please...''

His eyes narrowed to dark slits, then he snatched up his boots and socks he'd brought downstairs with him and walked quietly out the back door.

Melanie smoothed a hand through her hair, then she sucked in a deep breath and walked into the living room, praying that they wouldn't see how badly her knees were shaking.

Ian was halfway up the stairs with a sleeping Kevin in his arms, Cara was right behind him.

''You're back early,'' Melanie said, forcing a light

tone to her voice. She knew that Gabe had parked in the back and hoped that neither Cara nor Ian had seen his truck.

"He fell asleep before cake and ice cream, so we just brought him back." Cara looked at her husband and said, "Lay him on the bed, and we'll be right there."

"Before ice cream?" Melanie furrowed her brow and watched Ian disappear into the upstairs bedroom. "My Kevin?"

Smiling, Cara came back down the stairs. "I think all the excitement just wore him out. The magician picked him out of the audience to help with one of his tricks, and he also played with the other kids in the rec room. He crawled into Ian's lap while the cake was being cut, and the next thing we knew he was out."

Good heavens. Melanie glanced up at the bedroom and frowned. That certainly wasn't like her son, she thought. But his nap had been short today, she reasoned, plus it had been a long time since he'd played with other kids. He also would have been excited when he'd been chosen as part of the magic act, which would have contributed to his exhaustion.

But to miss cake and ice cream? That was still unusual.

She looked back at Cara and smiled. "Thank you so much for taking him. It sounds like he had a wonderful time."

"He did, and we enjoyed it, too. He's a great kid." Cara glanced around the house as she came to the bottom of the stairs. "So, how was your evening?"

Melanie felt the heat rise to her cheeks. "Yes, it was...nice."

"Just nice?" Cara arched one brow. "Wasn't Gabe here?"

Good grief, but Cara was blunt, Melanie thought. There was certainly no beating around the bush with this woman.

Melanie nodded hesitantly. "He was here."

"Hmm. That doesn't sound good. Tell me if he's being a jerk, and I'll punch him out for you."

"I—I told him I was leaving in the morning."

"Oh." Cara drew in a deep breath. "You don't have to tell me how he took that. I know Gabe well enough."

"He was so angry with me." Melanie wrapped her arms tightly around her. She felt so cold inside. "I suppose he has a right to be."

"He cares about you. And Kevin." Cara touched her arm. "We all do, Melanie."

"I care about all of you, too," she said softly, and blinked back the threatening moisture in her eyes.

"Then stay," Cara said gently. "We won't let anyone hurt you or Kevin. We'd all be here for you both."

Desperately she wanted to say yes. She even considered it for one long, insane moment. If there was any way she could be sure that she and Kevin could be safe, and that no harm would come to these wonderful friends who only wanted to help her, she would say yes in a heartbeat.

But there were no guarantees. No assurances. Because if Vincent found her, she had no doubt that someone would be hurt.

She couldn't, *wouldn't* take that chance.

"I'm sorry, I can't."

Cara sighed. "If I thought it would do any good,

I'd stand here all night and argue, but it's your life, Mel, and I don't want to interfere. Just know that we're always here for you."

"Thank you." Melanie hugged Cara. "You have no idea how much that means to me."

Melanie glanced up and saw Ian watching her and Cara from the top of the stairs. For a split second, she saw something very dark and intense in his eyes, but then it was gone so quickly she wondered if she'd imagined it.

"I took his shoes off and covered him with a throw," Ian said as he strolled casually down the stairs. "He didn't even stir."

"A bolt of lightning wouldn't budge that kid from sleep," Melanie said with a smile.

"You go ahead and tuck him in," Cara suggested. "If you want, I'll go make us some coffee, and we can visit for a few minutes."

"I'd like that." She hesitated, then remembered that Gabe was still out back.

"Would you like Ian to ask Gabe to come back in?" Cara asked.

Melanie felt her face heat up. Dammit, she was blushing again. "You saw his truck?"

Cara grinned. "Just a lucky guess."

In spite of herself, Melanie laughed, then quickly sobered. It wasn't a good idea to see him again tonight. It was too soon. Everything between them was still too raw, too open.

"Will you tell him that I said good-night and that I'll see him in the morning."

To say goodbye.

"I'll send Ian." Cara gave Melanie a hug. "Why don't you check on Kevin while I make the coffee."

Forcing herself to think about Kevin and not her aching heart, Melanie hurried up the stairs. She paused at the top and glanced at the open door to Mildred's bedroom. Her hand tightened on the top rail as she remembered how she and Gabe had made love.

If only, she thought, then shook her head and went to take care of her son.

"What do you mean, 'The Sarbanes woman spotted me'?" Vincent hissed furiously into the phone as he paced back and forth beside the Van Camp pool. After a long day with Louise bitching at him and still no word on the phone records for Melissa's friend, Vincent had at least been looking forward to a swim. Something told him he was going to be deprived of even that small indulgence.

This Sarbanes woman was turning out to be as big a pain in the butt as Melissa.

"What the hell were you doing, you stupid moron," Vincent snapped, "dancing naked in front of her apartment?"

"No, Vinnie, I swear," Pinkie Pascal whined from a pay phone outside the bathrooms at The Bare Club Bar. Hard rock music from the dance floor vibrated the cracked plaster walls, and a volley of male shouts and whistles encouraged Miss Lolly Pop to remove the sailor shirt she'd worn for tonight's performance. Pinkie shot a glance at the well-endowed woman, then quickly turned his attention back to the telephone. "I was careful, boss, really careful, but all of a sudden these two cops are hassling me, asking me what I've been doing hanging around and why."

Idiots, Vincent thought and his hand tightened on the phone. He was surrounded by idiots. "And why does that mean the Sarbanes woman spotted you?" Vincent asked. "How do you know it wasn't a neighbor who reported some ugly guy hanging around?"

Pinkie had to raise his voice over the cheers from the audience. "'Cause I went back that night, you know, changed my clothes, wore a hat, then just sort of watched from a distance, and guess who comes out all dolled up in high heels and a tight dress."

Patience, Vincent thought angrily, dealing with stupid people required patience. "Who came out?" Vincent asked through clenched teeth.

"The Sarbanes woman," Pinkie said breathlessly. "I hadn't got a real good look at her before then, but hot *damn* is that one knockout woman. I swear my eyeballs melted just looking at her and—"

"Dammit, Pinkie," Vincent shouted into the phone. Enough with patience. "If you don't tell me something I want to hear right now, I'm going to fly to Boston myself and rip out your damn liver."

"She was with one of the cops that hassled me," Pinkie said excitedly. "She was hanging on his arm like they were best friends. So the way I see it—"

"She knows about us," Vincent finished for Pinkie. "She'd probably been watching for us, then got cozy with the cops so they would bust you. Dammit!" He kicked a lawn chair and sent it flying. "If she went to all that trouble, then that means she's been in touch with Melissa."

And if she'd been in touch with Melissa, Vincent thought, then the women must have some kind of plan.

"Do you want me to keep watching her?" Pinkie asked hopefully. The money had been enough to keep him in booze and women and a little extra playtime with his bookie, too. "I'll keep out of sight, she won't even—"

"You're done." Vincent stood at the edge of the Van Camp pool and stared at the sparkling blue water. The smell of chlorine filled the warm, Southern California night air. "Get your butt back here now."

He clicked off the portable phone and tossed it onto a lounge chair.

He'd only been guessing that Melissa might contact her old friend, reaching for any and all long shots. It seemed that this one had paid off, even though the Sarbanes woman had outsmarted them this time.

He needed those phone records, dammit. His contact at the phone company had been dragging his feet, but Vincent knew that everyone had their price. He'd just have to double the inducement he'd already offered. He was certain there would be a number in those records that would lead him to Melissa.

And if he didn't get that phone log in a few days, then maybe he'd just have to go pay this Raina Sarbanes a visit himself. Convince her to tell him where Melissa was hiding.

Vincent narrowed his eyes and smiled. "I'm coming for you, Melissa, baby. Any day now, it's you and me."

Invigorated by the thought, he dived into the warm water and swam.

Chapter 9

By seven-thirty the next morning, Gabe had prepared himself for a fight. He'd spent half the night in his garage beating the hell out of his punching bag, and the other half pacing while he cursed Melanie and her damn stubborn streak. He'd also gone a few rounds with Jack Daniel's, but even that hadn't eased the storm raging inside him. He'd showered and shaved, and for the past hour he'd simply been driving around, mentally preparing himself for a confrontation with Melanie.

She wasn't going anywhere, dammit. He wouldn't let her.

He'd nearly taken some of his frustration out on Ian last night when his brother-in-law had come outside and talked to him while Cara and Melanie had coffee in the house. Gabe had intended to wait until his sister and brother-in-law had left, then go back in and have it out with Melanie. Ian had quickly recognized Gabe's mood and told him to go home and come back in the morning when he'd calmed down. In two short words, Gabe had told Ian what he thought of that idea, but in his gut Gabe knew that Ian was right and he'd finally—reluctantly—given in.

Still, he hadn't left quietly. Dirt and gravel had flown in all directions as his truck had roared down the driveway, and he'd downshifted so hard he'd ground out second gear. Costly and childish, but he'd had to do *something* to release the frustration gripping him or he would have gone back in the house and done something really stupid—like tie her up or lock her in the basement.

Even now, with the rise of dawn, he still hadn't ruled out those options.

With a death-grip on his steering wheel, he turned into the driveway and parked behind the house as he always did. He drew in a long, deep breath and stepped out of his truck, then quickly ducked into the side door of the garage to make sure her car was still here. He'd known it would be, of course, because he'd disconnected her coil wire the night before. Heavy-handed, but he felt no guilt. He wasn't taking any chances that she might have left before they talked.

Her hood was up.

Dammit. So she *had* tried to leave.

Furious, he spun on his heels, muttering curses as he headed for the house. Leaves crunched under his boots; his balled fists swung at his sides. He'd told himself all the way over here that no matter what, he'd be calm, but firm. Logical, but insistent. Now that he was here all he wanted to do was shout.

Clenching his jaw, he was reaching for the back

door when it flew open and Melanie stood there. Panic etched her face; her eyes were bright with moisture.

"Gabe! Thank God you're here!"

He opened his mouth, but she had already turned and was dashing back through the kitchen, then disappeared into the living room.

What the hell?

Frowning, he hesitated, then started to follow, but she burst back through the door with Kevin in her arms. They were both dressed and wearing their jackets. Her son lay limply in her arms, with his flushed face pressed against her chest.

"He woke up half an hour ago with a fever," she choked out. "I tried to call you, but there was no answer, and then my car wouldn't start and I didn't know how—"

"Give him to me."

Equal doses of shame and fear shot through him, but he'd deal with both emotions later. He reached for Kevin, gently pulled him from his mother's arms into his own, and headed for the door. Kevin whimpered softly, and Gabe felt the burn of the child's hot skin against his own neck.

Melanie hurried to the truck, buckled herself in, then took her son back into her arms and settled him against her while Gabe climbed in and started the truck. The engine roared to life and Gabe headed for Bloomfield County Emergency.

"I should have seen the signs. He had a short nap and was so cranky when he woke up, then last night he fell asleep before ice cream and cake." Melanie rocked a very still Kevin in her arms, pressed her lips to his forehead. "He gets ear infections from time to time, but he hasn't had one for a while. I was hoping that he'd outgrown them."

Kevin cried softly and put his hand to his ear. Gabe felt as if a knife were ripping through his chest. As far as sickness went, his brothers had all been old enough to take care of themselves after their parents had died. Cara had been a teenager, but other than a mild case of the flu and a sprained ankle, she'd been self-sufficient, too. He'd never dealt with a young child being sick before, never experienced this gripping sense of helplessness.

He concentrated on the road, drove fast, but carefully, and held his jaw so tight he thought his teeth might crack.

Melanie murmured softly to Kevin, then looked up suddenly. "Gabe, I'm sorry, but I may not have enough money for—"

"Don't say it." He stopped her, wanted to be angry that she would even hesitate to think he wouldn't take care of Kevin. But he couldn't be angry with her about anything at the moment. "Don't even think about it," he said gently. "Please."

He glanced at her, felt his throat thicken as he watched a single tear slide down her soft cheek. It was the first time he'd seen her cry, and the sight of it clawed at his insides.

They reached the hospital in record time and Kevin was taken in immediately. The doctor confirmed that Kevin did indeed have an ear infection, as Melanie had thought. A bad one, but not serious. An antibiotic and pain medication was prescribed, plus lots of rest and a recheck in one week. A lollipop from the nurse almost brought a smile to Kevin's lips, and when Gabe gathered the sick child back into his arms and carried him to the truck, he knew his heart was lost forever.

She made the coffee strong, poured it black and steaming into a mug, then set the cup on the kitchen table in front of Gabe. "Can I make you some breakfast?"

He shook his head. "Melanie, he's asleep now, just sit down for a minute."

Kevin's fever had started to drop soon after he'd taken his medication, and he'd closed his eyes the minute Gabe had laid him on the sofa in the living room. Melanie had tucked a soft blue blanket around her son, slipped his favorite teddy bear under his arm, then come out in the kitchen and made coffee.

"It wouldn't be any problem." She was too keyed up not to do something. "I've got eggs and bacon, or some pancakes—"

"Melanie, sit down." Gabe reached out and took hold of her wrist, then tugged her onto the kitchen chair. "You look exhausted."

She could only imagine what she looked like after less than two hours' sleep last night and then the ordeal with Kevin this morning. She glanced at Gabe, saw the red tinge in the whites of his eyes and the heavy droop of his lids. "So do you."

He rose, poured her a cup of coffee, then set it in front of her as he sat back down at the table. "We could both use a jump start."

"Thank you." Not certain what to do with her hands, she wrapped them around the hot mug. The heat felt good against her cold fingers. "I don't know what I would have done if you hadn't shown up when you did," she said quietly.

"You could have called Lucian or Reese or Callan and Abby. And Cara and Ian, of course, but they're farther away." He leaned forward, softened his voice. "We're all here for you and Kevin."

His words made her eyes burn with tears, and she quickly blinked them away. "I know, and that means more to me than you can imagine. It's just...been a long time since I've asked anyone for help." She glanced up and smiled weakly. "I'm out of practice."

She saw the question in his eyes, but he didn't ask. He just waited.

Closing her eyes on a sigh, she sat back in her chair, felt the weariness seep into her bones. "I was only eleven when my father died," she said softly, then opened her eyes and stared at the steam rising from her coffee. "My mother had a difficult time meeting the bills, but mostly she just hated not having a man to take care of her. She remarried when I was fourteen to a dentist who didn't want children, especially another man's. I was in the way, so I spent most of my teenage years at my friend Raina's house. After high school, Raina went away to college, but I stayed local. I was working as a salesclerk at an antique store to support myself and pay for school. That's where I met my husband. He'd come into the store looking for a birthday present for his mother."

It felt like a lifetime, she thought, though it had only been six years ago. Six long, life-altering years.

"He was handsome and charming, and he said he'd keep coming back every day until I agreed to go out with him," Melanie said wistfully. "On the fifth day I finally did agree, but it was our third date before I found out that he was also wealthy."

She watched Gabe's face harden, and she couldn't

help but smile. "I didn't marry him for his money. In fact, I turned him down several times because of it. We were from completely different backgrounds, and I knew his family didn't approve of me. I realized much later, of course, that was partly why he was so determined to marry me. I was his own personal revenge against his parents for dominating his life. That, and the fact that I wouldn't sleep with him. Phillip was a man who was used to getting what he wanted. For him, sex had nothing to do with love."

"And for you?" Gabe picked up his coffee, took a sip while he watched her over the rim.

"I was young and naive," she said with a shrug. "Phillip could be very charming when he wanted something and I thought he loved me. I was certain I loved him. But I realized later it was about security, about being taken care of, just as it had been with my mother. If she hadn't died in my second year of college, I know she would have been thrilled I was marrying into money. She would have considered that extremely successful."

"What did you consider it?"

He'd asked the question calmly, but Melanie heard the underlying tension in Gabe's voice. He needed to know about Phillip, she understood, just as much as she realized she needed to tell him.

"We were happy for the first year," she said, drawing in a long breath, "though we did disagree about my working. He won, of course. He always won. He wanted me home, like one of his possessions." She lifted her coffee cup, set it back down without taking a sip. "Then I got pregnant and everything changed."

Gabe frowned at her. "He didn't want children?"

"He insisted I have an abortion."

Gabe's knuckles went white on his coffee cup, and he slowly lowered it to the table. Melanie nearly shivered from the black violence that glinted sharply in his eyes. What he called her ex-husband was unrepeatable in front of children and gentle ears, but quite accurate, Melanie thought.

"Whatever love I felt for Phillip died at that moment," she said evenly. "He told me he wanted to wait, and that after we'd had more time alone together we would have children. But I still refused to do it, of course. It was the first time I'd defied him, and he was furious. In my fifth month of pregnancy, when I started to show, he stayed away from the house a lot, on the pretense of working or traveling, but we both knew he simply didn't want to be around a fat, pregnant woman. I suspected an affair, but wasn't certain until after Kevin was born. I threatened to leave him, but he swore it was nothing and it would never happen again."

Other than what she'd had to tell her lawyer, Melanie had never told anyone about her marriage. It almost felt as if she were telling someone else's story. The wife wronged, the cheating, overbearing husband. It was all so pathetic.

And yet, strangely, she wasn't humiliated telling Gabe. She felt lighter somehow, more free than she had in a very long time.

She moistened her lips, stared at her coffee cup and continued, "When Kevin was finally old enough for me to work part-time, I defied Phillip again and went back to work with a large antique company handling acquisitions and auctions. I loved the work, and since I could take Kevin with me most of the time, it was perfect for me. Phillip and I rarely even saw each other. I was busy with work, and he was busy with his latest girlfriend.''

Gabe swore, shook his head. ''Why didn't you just leave the bastard?''

''I finally did, even got my own place, but my mother-in-law convinced me that Phillip was just acting out his grief over his father's recent death and that with a little therapy he'd be fine. As difficult as it was, I still thought that because he was the father of my baby, he had certain rights and that I should try to make it work, no matter what. So I went back.''

She sighed, ran a hand through her hair. ''When the affairs continued, I finally realized that staying was doing more harm than good to Kevin and me, and I filed for divorce. He refused to give me one, of course, and fought me with his high-priced lawyers. He wasn't one to admit he was wrong, and he wasn't about to let go without making it very messy. It surprised us both that I hung in there and refused to come back to him.''

Gabe's chair screeched across the wooden floor as he stood. He moved stiffly to the counter, reached for the coffeepot, then slammed it back down and turned to face her. ''I'd like to get my hands on that son of a—''

''Gabe,'' she cut him off. ''He's dead.''

He stilled, then stared at her so hard she started to laugh. ''I didn't kill him, if that's what you're thinking. He was killed in a boating accident.'' Her smile faded as she shook her head. ''I will admit, though, I was tempted several times.''

Melanie watched Gabe rake his hands through his hair, and in spite of the moment, in spite of the conversation, she couldn't help but remember how she'd ran her own fingers through that thick, dark hair only last night. Her fingers itched now to touch him again, to feel his strength under her hands, to feel him move inside her.

But she couldn't. She didn't dare. She had no regrets about last night, but it would be different now. He already had her heart, but if they made love again, he'd have her very soul. She'd never be able to leave him then.

And she had to leave, for his sake, as well as Kevin's and her own.

"If he's dead," Gabe asked, "then who the hell are you running from?"

If she told him everything, her real name, about Louise Van Camp and Vincent Drake, she knew that there was no way Gabe would let it rest. He would want to take care of it for her. And she couldn't let him do that, wouldn't risk any harm coming to him.

"Don't ask me that, Gabe," she said softly. "It's the one thing I can't tell you. But I will tell you that Kevin and I need to start over. Just the two of us. It's the only way we'll ever be safe."

His face hardened. "There's always another way."

She shook her head, felt her eyes start to droop as the adrenaline rush she'd been on began to wane. "I'll be here for another week, until Kevin is better. Right now, let's just take each day as it comes."

She knew he wanted to argue, she saw it in the narrowing of his eyes and the tight press of his lips. But he wasn't going to. Not now, at least, and even though she knew it was because of Kevin, she was extremely thankful for the reprieve.

He pushed away from the counter and moved toward her. "Come on—" he gently took hold of her shoulders and lifted her out of the chair "—let's go upstairs."

In spite of her exhaustion, she pulled away from him. "Gabe, I can't—we can't, I mean—"

He shook his head and sighed. "I mean *all* of us, Kevin and you and me. It was a long night, and a rough morning. We're both too exhausted to think about anything but sleep right now. I just want to lay down and hold you."

He pressed his mouth to her temple, and she closed her eyes at the soft touch of his lips on her skin. Her shoulders sagged in his hands.

"Okay?" he asked, then slid his finger over her cheek and tucked a strand of hair behind her ear.

How long had it been since someone—a man—had wanted to just hold her? Melanie wondered. Maybe never, she realized, and felt tears burn her eyes again, not certain if they were tears of joy or anguish.

Both, she decided as she gazed up at him and whispered, "Okay."

The painters finished the exterior of the Witherspoon house on Monday, cleaned up and were gone by Tuesday, and by Wednesday afternoon a crew of landscapers had mowed and edged the lawn, pruned all the shrubs and replanted the front and back flower beds with warm fall colors.

The place looked good, Gabe thought as he walked the perimeter of the house. Damn good, in fact, if he did say so himself. There was still work to do inside; paint the walls and refinish the wood floors. But those things, plus the other odds and ends repairs that he needed to do, would have to wait until after the auction on Saturday. Most of the contents would be sold then, and whatever was left and couldn't be used at the center would be boxed and carted away.

And then the house would be empty.

He dragged a hand over his face and frowned darkly.

Gabe had kept a careful distance from Melanie these past few days. He was afraid that even the slightest, most innocent touch might push him over the edge, and he'd lose control. Take her to the closest bed and make love to her the way he desperately wanted to.

Of course, a child in the house seriously forestalled any action that Gabe might have wanted to take in that department, not to mention workmen all over the place. But he could have come back at night, late, when it was quiet, when Kevin was sleeping. He could have come to her then, kissed her until she trembled in his arms the way she had before.

But he hadn't. He'd gone to the tavern every night instead. Shared a beer with Reese and Lucian, watched a couple of games, argued over who would go to the World Series and who was better looking, Lucian or Reese. The same old nonsense he'd enjoyed his entire life. Only it felt different now.

It felt…hollow. Flat.

For the first time in his life he wanted more. He wasn't certain what "more" was, but he knew it involved Melanie and Kevin.

She might think that he had accepted her leaving, that after she'd explained her asinine, controlling husband and his family that he would understand her need to break all ties with that life and be completely independent now.

But she was wrong. He most certainly hadn't given

up. And though he knew there was more she wasn't telling him, he hadn't pushed that issue, either. He'd find out soon enough. It was taking a little longer than he'd expected, but armed with what little information they had, Ian would have a file on Melanie before the week was over.

Gabe stopped, hands on his hips and looked out over the cornfields behind the house. The sky was deep blue overhead, the air warm, heavy with the scent of fall. The leaves would be changing soon, and the landscape would be a riot of reds and golds and oranges. He wanted Melanie and Kevin to see that, to share that amazing sight with him. But if he couldn't change Melanie's mind, if he couldn't persuade her to stay in Bloomfield, then he'd be watching those leaves all by himself.

The thought made his chest tighten.

"What'cha looking at?"

Gabe turned at the sound of Kevin's voice. Dressed in jeans and tennis shoes and his Batman T-shirt, he stood on the back porch, a baseball in one hand, a mitt in the other—a get-well gift that Gabe had brought him. Actually one of several presents he'd brought him, in spite of Melanie's protests. Two hours in the toy section at the department store—hey, a guy had to play a little, didn't he?—and three big bags later, he'd shown up at the house. Melanie had insisted he take everything back except for one storybook, then quietly told him that she didn't have room for everything in her car. It was all he could do not to shake her and tell her she wasn't going anywhere.

But to shake her would mean he'd have to touch

her, and if he touched her, he'd have to kiss her, and if he kissed her, then he'd have to—

Well, hell. He didn't want to have thoughts like that while her son was staring so innocently at him.

But the bottom line was, Gabe had taken the toys with him that night, and had been bringing them back, one or two presents each day. He knew that Melanie wanted to strangle him, he just didn't care. The pleasure on Kevin's face every day was worth it.

Gabe smiled at the boy. "I'm just looking at the cornstalks. How you doin', partner?"

"I'm all better, but I still have to take that yucky pink medicine. My mom says I'm not supposed to bother you."

"You're not bothering me." *It's your mother who bothers me, who I can't stop thinking about.* "I'm done working for the day."

"My mom's not." Kevin tossed the ball up, tried to catch it, then scrambled after it when it dropped. "She found a boxful of old stuff in the basement and got all excited about it. She's been typing at her computer ever since and talking to herself. Why are you looking at a bunch of corn?"

"Just remembering when I was a kid." Gabe walked over, scooped Kevin up in his arms and walked to the edge of the field. The scent of ripe corn and damp earth filled the warm air. "My brothers and I used to play hide-and-seek in cornfields. Sometimes we'd each build a fort and play soldier. We'd fight each other, then bomb the forts with dirt clods."

Kevin's eyes opened wide. "My mom says I'm not allowed to fight or throw things. She says someone could get hurt."

Oops. Gabe hadn't quite gotten used to what he

could or couldn't say in front of kids. Mothers didn't like their kids throwing dirt clods. Dads, of course, understood completely.

"Your mom's right. We just did it once," he lied, then told a partial truth. "Callan got hit in the head with a big one, and there was blood all over the place. My mom found out, we got in big trouble and she grounded us all for a year."

"A whole year!"

"Something like that," Gabe said. He thought it was actually a weekend. "We were just little kids, so we had to learn you shouldn't do that."

Kevin stared hard at Gabe. "Were you ever little, like me?"

"Sure I was. And my brothers were, too."

Kevin stared at the cornfields. "I want to be big like you. I'd make him go away and not hurt my mommy."

Gabe went still, then very slowly, very carefully, said, "Who would you make go away?"

"That bad man. He's mean and ugly, and I hate him."

Kevin's eyes narrowed sharply, and it twisted Gabe's gut to see a child possess such intense anger.

"How did he hurt your mommy?" Gabe asked gently, afraid of Kevin's answer, but desperately needing to know.

"He held her arms and pushed her, and he made her cry."

The image of this faceless coward touching Melanie and scaring Kevin made Gabe's heart stop. Never in his life had he felt such sheer, raw anger at another person. The desire to lash out overwhelmed him, but instead he reminded himself to breathe, to stay calm, to focus on Kevin.

"Do you know his name?" Gabe asked, knowing that Melanie would be furious at him for prying information out of her son. At the moment, he just didn't give a damn. He had to be certain, he needed to know that this wasn't something that had happened between Melanie and Kevin's father.

"Vincent," Kevin said fiercely. "His name is Vincent, and if he hurts my mommy again I'm going to kick him hard."

Vincent. It was a name, at least. Something to direct his rage at later, when he was alone.

But who the hell was he? And why was he after Melanie and Kevin?

Gabe slowly set Kevin down on the ground. "If he ever hurts you or your mommy, you kick him as hard as you can. Do you think you can remember if I show you how?"

Kevin looked up at Gabe, pressed his lips tightly together, then straightened his little body and nodded tightly. Once again Gabe felt a surge of emotion rip through his body. He swore that no one was ever going to hurt this child or his mother again.

"All right," Gabe said, and pointed toward his foot. "This is what you do…."

Chapter 10

Saturday dawned with the crisp, cool bite of autumn, but clear blue skies promised heat in the afternoon. The air was still, heavy with the tangy scent of maples and freshly turned earth, and the cheerful morning song of sparrows in a nearby oak tree greeted the truckloads of busy workers scattered across Mildred Witherspoon's front yard.

Melanie stood at the upstairs bedroom window, half listening to the sounds of her son playing with his action characters in the next room, while she watched all the activity below. Several men and women—most of them volunteers from the center—scurried around as they set up a large, puffy white tent and plastic folding chairs, while several others began assembling the items to be auctioned behind a tall podium.

Excitement shivered up her spine.

She'd always loved the day of an auction: the crew

setting up, the anticipation in the air, the competition between anxious buyers. They'd be coming soon; their sleek, fancy cars and glossy limousines would drive up the long, gravel driveway like thirsty cattle heading for the water hole. She leaned closer to the window, wishing desperately she could be a part of everything.

Simon Grill had arrived a little while ago, handsome as always in his tailored, steel-gray Armani suit, glossy black Ferragamo shoes and trademark red silk pocket scarf. His thick black hair, peppered with gray, was brushed back from his elegant face and piercing blue eyes. How she ached to run out and throw herself into his arms, to breathe in the scent of his familiar two-hundred-dollar-an-ounce cologne. He was a large man, tall and muscular, in his late thirties, an Ivy League sophisticate with a dry wit who openly disdained the wealthy, and bullied them into opening their pocketbooks with his blatant reproach. He'd fallen into auctioneering as a hobby and found he was good at it, better than good. Simon Grill was the best.

Not only as an auctioneer, Melanie thought as she watched him lovingly stroke a Duncan Phyfe writing desk with one large, manicured hand, but as a friend. He'd known about her trouble with Phillip, then Louise. He'd even offered to help, but she hadn't wanted to involve him. Simon's family had been longtime friends of the Van Camps, and it would have caused problems for him. And then after what had happened to Paul, and realizing what Vincent would do to anyone who helped her, Melanie had thought it best to just distance herself from everyone in the business. She couldn't bear to see anyone else hurt because of her.

She watched Simon as he moved from item to item, checking his list, making notes, then carefully examining each piece. He knew his antiques, and Melanie knew that with the dealers and collectors they had coming today, and the remarkable items up for sale, there would be a whirlwind of bidding.

With a sigh, she turned her attention to the other man she'd been watching this morning. The man who occupied her mind not only every waking minute, but her dreams, as well.

Gabe stood in the back of his pickup, handing folding chairs down to Callan and Reese. He wore dress jeans today, shiny black cowboy boots and a white button-up shirt with the sleeves rolled to his elbows. She drank in the sight of him, watched the ripple of sinew and muscle across his arms and shoulders as he swung chairs over the side of his truck. Her gaze drifted down his lean hips and long legs, and she remembered the feel of those powerful, strong legs against her own.

Her skin suddenly felt hot and tight, her breasts ached.

With his truck unloaded, he jumped easily over the side, and when he hit the ground, a shock of thick, dark hair fell onto his temple. The need to comb her fingers through those wayward strands overwhelmed her.

She wanted to go to him, to slip her arms around him and pull him close, to press her body and lips to his and tell him that she loved him.

Gabriel Sinclair had completely stolen her heart. Longing consumed her, and she desperately wished that things could be different, that she could stay here with him.

Wondered, in moments of insanity, if maybe she could.

He'd kept his distance from her this past week, and she knew he was waiting for her to come to him. How she'd wanted to. It had taken every last ounce of willpower not to reach out and touch him, to slip into the warmth and strength of his arms, to hold him in the dark of night, when all was quiet and the demons that plagued her were at their loudest.

Before she'd come here, she was so certain what it was that she needed to do. But what had been so crystal clear to her before had now become cloudy. She was confused, and worse, she had doubts. The absolute had become questionable.

She'd been so careful, left everything behind her and severed all ties, meticulously covered her tracks all the way across the country. The only person she'd been in touch with at all had been Raina, and now even Raina didn't know where she was or where she was going.

She didn't know where she was going. With Vincent watching for her in Boston, she certainly couldn't go there now.

She knew she was going to have to settle somewhere in the next few months. Did she dare stop so soon? Bloomfield County was a small town, exactly the type of place she would have chosen to live. She could find a job close by, something inconspicuous.

And Gabe was here. The ache in Melanie's chest tightened. He was both a blessing and a curse. She'd already fallen in love with him, and she knew Kevin was crazy about him, too. But she knew if they stayed, that Gabe would want to take care of them. She couldn't allow herself to become dependent on anyone. She might let her guard down, become too relaxed. All she had to do was make one mistake, one small error, and Louise would find them.

Vincent would find them.

She squeezed her eyes shut. As much as she wanted to, she couldn't stay here. Wishful thinking, that's all this was. Foolish thinking.

Her breath caught as she watched Gabe approach Simon. Gabe knew that she had worked with the auctioneer, that they'd been friends. She'd made it clear from the beginning that no one could know she was here—especially Simon—and now she worried if Gabe would respect her need for anonymity. It didn't matter that Simon didn't know her as Melanie Hart, a few questions from Gabe about a woman and her young son named Kevin and Simon would know instantly.

Her fingers curled tightly around the lace curtain as Gabe shook Simon's hand.

As she watched the men speak, she relaxed her grip on the curtains and slowly released the breath she'd been holding. Gabe wouldn't say anything. She knew he wouldn't. The man might drive her crazy, but she was certain he wouldn't expose her or Kevin to danger.

"Melanie! Where are you? Is this just too wonderful!"

Melanie turned at Cara's cheerful greeting and watched as she flounced into the bedroom, carrying a brown leather suitcase.

"They're already waiting to come in, and we won't even be open for an hour." Cara was flushed the same rosy color as the silk blouse she wore under her crisp navy suit. Excitement glowed from her face. "Ian and

Lucian are standing guard down at the front gates to keep everyone out until we're ready."

"I hope they're heavily armed," Melanie said with a smile. "You never know when these crowds can turn ugly."

Melanie's smile faded slightly when another woman, a petite platinum blonde with short spiked hair and huge violet eyes, followed Cara into the room. The woman's black skirt was long and snug, her spandex long-sleeved top cut high to expose a flat midriff. She was also carrying a suitcase.

"Melanie, this is Ivy." Cara set her suitcase down. "Ivy, Melanie."

"Hey," Ivy said, the single word heavy with a New York Italian accent. She set her suitcase down, as well.

Melanie nodded politely. Both Cara and Ivy moved closer. "So what do you think?" Cara asked.

Ivy folded her skinny arms and narrowed her eyes. "Piece a cake."

Melanie stiffened. Who the hell was this woman to call her a piece of cake? "Excuse me?"

Cara and Ivy flanked her. Ivy leaned close and stared hard. Melanie shifted uncomfortably.

"I'd kill for her skin," Ivy said as if Melanie wasn't even there. "And it'll be a shame to cover up that gorgeous hair. People pay big bucks for hair like that."

Melanie's hand instinctively reached up and touched the ends of her hair. What on God's earth was she talking about? And if this woman lifted one finger to her hair, Melanie thought, she'd flatten her.

"Can you have her ready in time?" Cara asked.

"A snap." Ivy turned and headed for the suitcases.

"Ready?" Melanie glanced anxiously from Cara to Ivy. "Have me ready for what?"

Both Cara and Ivy looked at her now, both smiled slowly.

"Honey," Ivy said in her deep, smoky voice. "I'm gonna make you a new woman."

"I have two thousand," Simon boomed out from the podium. "Two thousand for these amazing Edwardian sterling silver cherub candlesticks. Do I hear twenty-five, twenty-five—" He pointed his gavel and waved it as if he were maestro over an orchestra. "Yes! I have twenty-five to number eleven. Do I hear twenty-seven?"

The spicy scent of freshly crushed apples from the cider stand drifted on the cool morning air and mixed with the sweet smell of just-baked muffins, breads and pies. There were other enticing aromas, as well: caramel apples, warm cinnamon rolls, hot chocolate. Gabe's stomach rumbled as he folded his arms and leaned against a porch column to watch the show from the front of the house.

And what a show it was.

The cast of players—namely the buyers—who'd come from as far away as England and Germany, were the most interesting part of the performance. Most of the nearly three hundred people present were blatantly wealthy. The men wore expensive, tailored suits and Rolex watches, while the women wore elegant silk dresses and diamonds the size of baseballs. Men and women alike sat stiff as fence posts, with bored, disinterested expressions on their faces. Gabe wondered if a loose rat under the chairs might liven things up a bit.

The auction had opened maybe twenty minutes ago, but already this guy Simon had prodded close to thirty thousand dollars from the audience. He talked the same as he looked: fast and smooth. And with his refined good looks, Gabe supposed that women found the guy attractive, as well.

He'd been chewing on that thought since he'd met the man, wondering what the relationship between Melanie and this Simon was, or had been, but it was a big bite he couldn't seem to swallow. He knew they were friends, but he couldn't stop thinking that they might be more. The auctioneer had been friendly enough, and though he had an air of detachment about him, Gabe had the distinct feeling that the guy was keenly aware of everything and everyone around him.

Gabe listened to Simon describe the next item up for bid, a nineteenth-century oil painting by an artist Gabe had never heard of. He watched the auctioneer work the crowd, badger them and squeeze the price up until their eyes nearly bulged. He was good, Gabe had to admit. Damn good. He didn't like the idea of Melanie with this guy one little bit. But then, he realized, he didn't like the idea of Melanie with *any* guy other than him.

He'd been too busy helping set up this morning to talk to her or her son, but he knew Kevin was playing upstairs with a few other kids from the center and that Melanie was probably watching the auction from a bedroom window.

He knew how much she'd wanted to be out here, to be a part of the auction. Someone had taken away everything from her, forced her to give up the life that she'd enjoyed so much, her friends, her home.

Forced her to run away and hide, to be afraid. Gabe didn't know why, but he did know who.

Vincent. Gabe had no idea who the man was, but he did know he couldn't wait to meet up with him. He couldn't wait to show the bastard what he thought of men who bullied women and children. Soon, Gabe thought as he narrowed his eyes. They'd be meeting soon.

Ian had told him this morning that his contact in Washington had pulled together a file on Melanie, and Ian thought that he'd have the information tonight. Gabe had no plan as to what he would do with that information once he had it, but he'd damn well do *something.* If she hated him for interfering, then so be it. He wasn't about to stand around and do nothing. He couldn't. Somehow, someway, he was going to help her and Kevin—whether she liked it or not.

And she wouldn't, of course. That was a given.

From the corner of his eye, he noticed Cara watching him from one of the food stands. In fact, for the past few minutes, every time he'd glanced her way, he'd noticed her watching him. He wondered why she'd suddenly gained such an interest in him.

She was up to something, but he'd be damned if he knew what it was.

"Hey, handsome, care to buy a lady a drink?"

He turned at the warm-as-smooth-whiskey Southern drawl behind him.

Good God.

The woman was hot enough to fry any man's brain. Her hair was the palest blond, short and shaggy around a porcelain-smooth face. Her charcoal-smudged eyes were huge, her wide, sensual lips deep-dark red, accented by a tiny mole above one tilted up corner. He couldn't stop his gaze from traveling downward to the lush cleavage at the deep V of her tight burgundy sweater, down to the narrow waist of her snug black skirt, then lower still, down her impossibly long curvy legs to her glossy black high heels.

His heart slammed in his chest. In spite of the fact that she wasn't the woman he wanted, he gave her a long look of appreciation. He was flesh and blood, after all.

When his gaze returned to the woman's face, when he noticed the deep, smoke-colored eyes, a warning bell sounded loudly in his brain.

He'd been had.

"Darlin'," he drawled right back, "with a body like that, I'll buy you anything you want."

The woman's enticing smile dipped a fraction, then lifted again as she stepped closer. She smelled exotic, Gabe noted. Something that made a man think of hot, hard sex.

She reached out and ran a long, blood-red nail up his arm. "But you don't know what I want," she purred. "And you don't know how much it will cost you."

"I know what you want, sweetheart." He brought his lips close to hers, hovered there as he whispered, "And I know exactly how much it will cost me."

Her eyes widened, then narrowed. With a sigh, she folded her arms and looked at him. "How did you know?"

He smiled, held her surprised gaze. "Those eyes of yours, darlin'. You could black out your front teeth and dress yourself in a clown suit and I'd know it was you.'' He reached out, lightly touched the fake mole with his fingertip. ''Nice touch.''

She frowned, glanced around longingly at all the people, then sighed. ''This was a bad idea. If you knew it was me, someone else might, too. I'll have to go back inside.''

''Hold on.'' He reached into the front pocket of his shirt, pulled out a pair of sunglasses, then slid them over her eyes. ''They might be a little big for you, but they'll do for now.''

He leaned toward her, lowered his mouth close to her ear. ''Now proposition me again in that hot little Southern accent. Damn if that didn't turn me on.''

Melanie shivered at the warm, brief brush of Gabe's lips on her earlobe. Heat spread through her body, seeped into her bones and made them feel soft. She'd never flirted like this before, certainly had never played the role of a tease. But Ivy's makeover had turned Melanie into some kind of a femme fatale. She felt sensuous and desirable and incredibly sexy.

Shameless, and maybe just a little bit indecent.

And because she was with Gabe, she also felt turned on.

The sound of Simon's voice calling out bids faded in the background, as did the throng of people around them. She felt herself sway toward him, felt her lips part as she lifted her face to his.

His deep green eyes darkened, then narrowed dangerously. ''Sweetheart, I've kept my hands off you for a week and it's nearly killed me. If you keep looking at me like that, I'm going to drag you into that house, find an empty room and do everything that I've been thinking about for the past six days.''

It was on the tip of her tongue to ask him to describe, in detail, what those things were, then do each and every one of them to her. When she suddenly remembered where she was, she jerked back and felt the burn of her blush. Good heavens! She'd practically begged him to take her, right here, in plain sight of everyone!

"I—I'm sorry," she stammered. "I wasn't thinking. I got a little caught up in...my disguise."

"Shouldn't a disguise make you *less* noticeable?" he asked, letting his gaze roam over her once again. "You could start a riot looking like this."

Melanie couldn't stop the thrill that coursed through her as Gabe stared at her with such open lust. "Ivy said I should look the opposite of how people would usually see me. Since I normally dress conservative, especially at an auction, this is about as opposite as it gets."

His gaze dropped to her low-cut neckline, then back up to her face. He arched a brow at her, but said nothing. She felt her blush deepen. "Ivy also said that a little cleavage would, uh, divert attention from my face."

"Ivy was certainly right about that." Gabe drew in a deep breath. "But it also makes me want to punch out every guy here who looks at you. Which, at the moment—" he scanned the audience behind him "—includes at least two of my brothers. They look like they're about ready to drown in their own drool."

Melanie reached up and covered her chest with her hand as she looked out and noticed Reese and Lucian staring openly at her from the sidelines of the crowd. "This *is* a bad idea," she said weakly and started to back toward the front door.

He took her wrist, pulled her gently back. "You

just stick close to me, darlin'. I'll handle crowd control." His grin was crooked as he tucked her hand neatly under his arm. "Now about that drink you wanted—hot apple cider or lemonade?"

The warmth and strength of his body against hers gave her courage and she relaxed against him, then fell back into her disguise and gave a coquettish tilt of her head. "Why, sugar," she drawled, "you know I like my drinks hot, just like my men."

He closed his eyes on a low, deep groan, then shook his head and chuckled. "Lord, I think this is going to be a long day." He leaned close and whispered into her ear. "And an even longer night, sweetheart."

She shivered at the thought of a long night with Gabe. Could she resist him?

Did she want to?

She didn't know anymore. She couldn't think with him so close, couldn't be logical or rational—didn't want to be. It felt good to be on Gabe's arm, to flirt and drink cider and nibble on the caramel apple he'd insisted on buying for her. She smiled and nodded at people she'd known for years, and not one of them had a clue who she was. Even Lloyd Withers, the lecherous little buyer for Marple and Barnes who'd been hitting on her for years, stared at her hard with his beady little eyes and didn't recognize her.

She stayed on the sidelines, oozed Southern charm and sensuality to keep in character with the role Ivy and Cara had created for her, enjoyed the excitement of the auction as Simon worked his magic on the crowd. She knew she'd have to avoid any contact with her friend, but she was happy to simply watch. It would possibly be years before she could once again be a part of this world she loved so much, and she wanted to savor every precious minute.

She felt lighter than she had in years, happy. Secure that for this one day, with Gabe at her side, she and Kevin would be safe.

By seven that evening, Simon and the buyers had left, the tent and folding chairs were loaded into the backs of Lucian's and Reese's pickups, and the volunteers had cleaned up and gone home. The warm day eased into a cool evening, and the scent of grilled food and pumpkin pies lingered in the air. A breeze swirled fallen leaves over the lawn where, only hours ago, fierce battles had raged in bidding wars between buyers and collectors.

They had left, most carrying their treasures with them, the victors smug, the losers indignant, both already anxious for the next battle at another auction.

For the Killian Shawnessy Foundation, the day had been most profitable.

Inside the house, the Sinclairs and Shawnessys gathered around the kitchen table. Melanie, still dressed in the same sweater and skirt, but minus her blond bombshell wig, makeup and sexy mole, joined in with the flurry of talk and laughter.

Gabe stood back, watching her. He'd never seen her as happy as she'd been today, so relaxed. There'd been a glow about her that had absolutely captivated him today. Of course, in that outfit she'd worn to the auction, she'd pretty much captivated every man there. Remembering the expressions on his brother's faces when he'd explained the blond bombshell on his arm was Melanie, and she was incognito for the day, Gabe chuckled to himself. Both Reese and Lucian were profoundly disappointed that the blonde wouldn't be going anywhere with either one of them.

She's mine, Gabe's expression had told his brothers and every other man who'd looked at Melanie. *All mine.*

"Okay, everybody, gather round." A silver bracelet of interlinking roses dangled from Cara's wrist as she handed out plastic flute glasses. Ian, with a loud pop, opened the champagne bottle and glasses were filled. Kevin beamed when he was given a flute of sparkling cider.

"A toast." Cara raised her glass. "To Melanie. For without her uncanny ability to recognize the common from the unique we would not have raised five hundred thousand dollars today."

There was a long moment of stunned silence, then the room broke into cheers and whistles. Callan hugged Abby while Lucian and Reese slapped each other on the back. Ian touched glasses with Cara, then tenderly kissed his wife and smiled.

Gabe took advantage of the moment to slip an arm around Melanie's waist and pull her close, then press his lips to hers. He heard her catch of breath, felt her mouth tremble against his, and it was all he could do not to drag her into his arms and kiss her the way he really wanted to.

At the moment, however, with Kevin and his family watching, it was hardly the time. He tightened his hold on her briefly, then released her.

Later, he told her with his eyes. *Later you are all mine.*

She blushed furiously, then looked quickly away as she sipped her champagne.

"You know, Lucian—" Reese had an evil grin on

his face as he set his champagne glass down on the table "—I do believe a proper Sinclair thank-you for Melanie is in order here, don't you?"

"Absolutely." Lucian set his glass down as well. "After you, bro."

"Stop that right now," Cara warned. Abby, who'd once been the recipient herself of the Sinclair males' nonsense—of which Gabe had been a participant, as well—simply rolled her eyes.

Grinning, Lucian and Reese ignored Cara and advanced on Melanie. Her eyes widened, and she started to take a step back, but they were too quick.

Reese snatched her into his arms and laid one on her.

Dammit! Gabe frowned darkly at his brothers; he should have seen this coming and headed it off before it got started. He pulled Reese away, but couldn't stop Lucian from slipping in and taking over where Reese had left off.

Melanie's eyes were wide and startled as Lucian kissed her, her palms flat on his chest.

"You know what they say," Gabe growled as he grabbed Lucian by the scruff of the neck and yanked hard.

"No." Lucian's eyes glinted with amusement as he squared off in front of Gabe. "What do they say?"

"'It's all fun and games until someone gets hurt.'" Gabe moved toward Lucian first. "Well, someone is about to get hurt."

"Knock it off, all three of you." Cara glared at Reese for starting it, then quickly stepped between Gabe and Lucian and put a hand on each of their chests. "You can all go outside and be stupid later. Right now we have another toast to make."

Gabe scowled at his brothers, then folded his arms and straightened. Melanie still look bewildered, but none the worse for wear, and Kevin, delighted by all the ruckus, bounced in his chair.

Cara moved back beside her husband, then glanced up at him and smiled broadly. He slid an arm around her waist and smiled right back.

Tears filled her eyes as she lifted her glass and looked around the room. "To the first Sinclair-Shawnessy child, who will make his, or her, appearance in approximately seven months' time."

Pandemonium broke out, and though Melanie stood by awkwardly for the first few moments, Gabe quickly pulled her into the celebration. This time, everybody kissed everybody and nobody minded. Kevin had no idea what all the fuss was about, but he giggled and squirmed as he was tossed around and soundly smooched.

When the celebration became a heated argument between the Sinclair brothers over who was not only the best-looking uncle, but the most intelligent, Cara threw up her hands and told everyone that she was exhausted and was taking her husband and going home.

"We were hoping you'd let us take Kevin tonight," Cara said quietly to Melanie while her son roughhoused with Reese. "One of our sponsors is hosting a pancake breakfast at the center tomorrow morning and there'll be games and prizes for the kids."

Gabe saw the fear flicker across Melanie's face, but then she looked at her son, watched him laugh and play, and those soft, sad eyes of hers suddenly turned sharp and bright. "Oh course you can take him. Thank you, he'll love it."

When they told Kevin he screamed with delight and ran upstairs to get his pajamas and toothbrush. The house quickly emptied after that. Callan and Abby were celebrating their three-month anniversary and had private plans; Reese and Lucian had a hot poker game going at the tavern, which, despite his brothers' taunting, Gabe declined to join.

He stood on the front porch and watched while Melanie waved goodbye to her son, watched her stare after the van until she could no longer see the tail-lights.

They were alone.

She turned slowly, lifted her gaze to his. He held out a hand to her. Keeping her eyes steady on his, she walked toward him.

Quimby Brothers of Beverly Hills specialized in custom men's suits and apparel. The store was small, but posh, and more than one celebrity frequented the exclusive shop. Their tailors were artists with fabric, their customers wealthy and demanding.

Hardly the sort of establishment that an ex-con from Reseda would ever consider patronizing.

Vincent stared into the full-length mirror in the fitting room, smiled as he tugged at the hem of his jacket. It had taken some fast talking to get Louise to buy him a suit from this joint, but because he was driving her to some stupid fund-raiser next week that everybody who was anybody would be at, she'd finally agreed. Appearances were everything to the old biddy, and Vincent had simply appealed to the woman's vanity.

"Would you care for a glass of white wine, sir?" the salesman asked and Vincent nearly glanced over his shoulder to see who the stuffy old geezer was talking to.

"Yeah, sure." Vincent stretched his neck and tugged at the hundred-dollar tie the old guy had picked out to go with the suit and dress shirt. What he really wanted was a cold beer, but what the hell.

He could get used to this, Vincent thought and stared at himself in the mirror. He was a good-looking guy. Maybe he'd pick himself up some high-class broad at one of those fund-raisers. Some lonely widow or divorcée with a truckload of dough. Then he wouldn't need that bitch Louise anymore.

She'd been harping on him every day that he hadn't found Melissa and Kevin yet. These things took time, dammit, but what would the lazy broad know about anything that had to do with work? If she wasn't getting her hair or nails done, she was at lunch or shopping while he did all her dirty work for her.

He glanced at his watch and frowned. He had to pick her up from the hair salon in twenty minutes, so these stuffed suits around here better shake a leg and finish hemming his pants.

Vincent was about to call for the salesman when the man suddenly reappeared with a phone in his hand. "Phone for you, sir."

Scowling, Vincent took the phone. Probably Louise already bitching at him to come pick her up. He dredged up his most congenial voice. "Vincent Drake here."

"It's not positive yet, boss," the man at the other end of the phone said. "But I think this is your lucky day."

Smiling at himself in the mirror, Vincent felt the adrenaline rush through his veins as he listened.

Ah, sweet Melissa, he thought, narrowing his eyes darkly as he stared at himself. We've found you at last.

Chapter 11

It surprised Melanie that she made it up the porch steps without stumbling. That she took Gabe's hand without hesitation. He pulled her to him, slipped an arm around her waist and tucked her close.

A full moon broke the tops of the trees while an owl hooted softly from a distant perch. The heady scent of fall leaves drifted softly on the cool night air.

With a sigh, Melanie rested her head on Gabe's strong chest, listened to the deep, heavy thud of his heart, breathed in the masculine scent of his skin. And felt more at peace than she had her entire life.

It didn't matter that it couldn't last. She would just take each moment as it came, and this moment was too precious to waste worrying about tomorrow.

She didn't want to even think about tomorrow. There was only now. Only tonight. She shivered with anticipation.

"Cold?" He ran his hands up her arms, then over her back. "We can go inside."

"In a minute." She turned in his arms, rested the back of her head against his wide chest as she stared out into the darkness. "My head is still spinning from the day."

"Five hundred thousand dollars is enough to make anyone's head spin," he said, resting his chin on the top of her head and wrapping his arms around her. "When that lamp went for seventy-five thousand dollars, I had to push my eyeballs back in their sockets."

"It's wasn't just a 'lamp,' Gabe," she said with a laugh. "I told you it was a signed Tiffany. I thought it would go for around sixty, but Simon was in rare form today. Every time I see him in action, I'm absolutely amazed."

She felt Gabe go very still, then she turned her head and glanced up at him.

"I hope," he said dryly, "the action you're referring to is his ability as an auctioneer."

He was jealous, she realized, and couldn't help but feel a tug of pleasure at the thought. "Simon and I are just friends," she said simply. "We've worked together on several projects, attended a lot of the same charity functions. I'm not his type."

"Sweetheart, you're every man's type," Gabe said firmly, then lifted his dark brows. "Oh. You mean he's gay."

She laughed at the absurdity of *that* thought. "Good grief, no. Simon Grill loves women. Your standard model, all-American playboy."

She turned, reached up and touched Gabe's cheek. It was rough with the faint stubble of beard, and she felt a tingle all the way from her fingertips down to her toes. She watched his eyes narrow and darken, saw the hunger rise.

He pulled her close, lowered his head to hers, lightly brushed his mouth against hers. Need hummed through her veins.

"I don't want to talk about Simon," he whispered, then nibbled on the corner of her mouth.

"Who?"

She felt his smile, then his lips covered hers in an all-consuming, mind-bending, swirling hot kiss. When he pulled away, Melanie felt herself sway toward him.

"Come inside with me," he murmured.

"Yes."

He took her hand, led her inside, then up the stairs, into the bedroom where they had first made love. Except for a large feather bed in the middle of the hardwood floor, the room was empty, most of the contents sold at the auction. Moonbeams streamed through the lace curtains on the windows and spilled across the walls like liquid silver.

Melanie's breath caught at the beauty of it, and when Gabe slid his hands through her hair and tilted her face up, she simply forgot to breathe.

His lips touched hers with such tenderness she felt tears come to her eyes. She'd never been treated with such care before, as if she were the most delicate flower, or the most fragile glass.

But underneath the softness, emotions simmered and strained. Underneath the gentleness, passion cried out, demanded to be released.

She moaned, curled her fingers into the cotton of his shirt, but still he took his sweet, sweet time.

Kissed her with a touch that was as light as a feather, but potent as black rum.

He slid his tongue over her lips, then inside to taste her more fully. She shuddered, opened to him, met the slow, steady dance of his mouth with her own. He tasted like sparkling champagne and caramel apple and hot desire.

She had to have her hands on him, his hands on her, or she'd die.

And then, as if he'd read her mind, his large, rough hands started to move. Down her back, over her hips, across the curve of her rear, where they tightened and pulled her intimately against his arousal. Heat poured through her veins and spread through her entire body like liquid fire. She trembled at his touch, slid her palms up his chest, over his strong shoulders. On a moan, he slanted his mouth harder against hers, deepened the kiss. Need coiled tightly inside her as if it were a fierce, living beast waiting to be released. It shocked her, this need, stunned her, made her heart hammer in her chest and her head spin with sensations too intense to control.

She jerked away, her breathing ragged, her pulse pounding in her temple as she lifted her gaze to his. Desire tightened his face and strong jaw, and the raw, primal need in his dark eyes sent a thrill skipping over her skin.

The room seemed to close around them as he waited, his breathing labored, his long, muscled body tense.

Holding his gaze with her own, Melanie took a step back, then reached for the hem of her sweater.

Gabe's heart slammed against his ribs.

Blood pumped through his veins, hot and wild. He

watched her pull her sweater over her head and had to remind himself to breathe. Black lace encased her high, firm breasts, shadows played over her smooth, pale skin, moonlight shimmered in her silky hair.

Her skirt slid down her long, curvy legs and pooled around her delicate ankles and feet. Still holding his gaze with hers, she stepped from the skirt.

More black lace, a mere sliver, stretched like a sultry smile from hip to hip.

The heat in his blood burst into flames.

He took a step toward her, stopped when she smiled slowly and shook her head.

"Your turn," she murmured.

Need ripped through his gut at her soft command. He fumbled blindly at the buttons on his shirt, felt one pop, heard the tiny bounce, then the roll of plastic on the hardwood floor. The sound echoed in the room.

The hiss of a zipper, the slide of denim, the drop of boots. And all the while she watched, her breasts rising and falling with her deep breaths, her hands moving restlessly over the curve of her hips and flat stomach. Like a warm, silk scarf, her gaze slid over his body, touched his shoulders, his arms, his chest, his belly, then dropped lower. Stopped. Her gray eyes molten.

She might as well have hit him with the frying pan again. He couldn't breathe, couldn't think, couldn't move. Pleasure swelled and pounded in his veins at the sight of her hungry eyes. He couldn't have been more aroused if she were actually touching him. He'd never experienced anything like this before. The wild beat of his heart felt like tribal drums awakening dark primal needs.

When she caught her bottom lip between her

straight white teeth, then drew in a slow, deep breath, his control broke.

His hand snaked out and dragged her against him.

His mouth covered hers, hard and deep. She met him with the same urgency, wound her arms around his neck as they came together in a frantic meeting of lips and tongue. Her breasts crushed against his chest, and she rose on tiptoe, squirming against him in her need to be closer. He cupped her rear end, squeezed hard, then turned so his body took the impact as they fell onto the feather bed. She landed on top of him with a small gasp, her hair brushing over his shoulders and chest like a curtain of velvet.

She was as greedy for him as he was for her. While her hands rushed over his chest, her mouth moved over his neck, tasting, nipping. Her fingernails raked through the hair on his chest, then her lips nibbled on the tiny nubs of his nipples. He closed his eyes on a groan, then sucked in a sharp breath when her mouth moved lower down his chest, across his belly…

He jerked up on an oath, grabbed her shoulders and rolled her onto her back, desperate to touch her, to be inside her.

Her hair fanned out around her face in dark, shimmering waves, her eyes, heavy-lidded and glazed with desire, stared up at him.

"You're beautiful," he murmured. "So beautiful."

"Touch me," she whispered. "Please touch me."

He wanted to, *needed* to, everywhere at once. He blazed kisses down the long, slender column of her throat, tasted the wild pulse at the base of her neck, dipped his tongue into the cove beneath her collarbone. Her skin was as warm and sweet as the fresh apple cider they'd had this morning, as heady as the champagne they'd had this evening. He was drowning in her, and still he couldn't get enough.

Her breath came in short gasps as he moved between the valley of her breasts. He cupped the soft lace-covered flesh in his hands, circled the pebbled tips of her nipples with his callused thumbs, watched the pleasure darken her eyes. When he flicked open the front clasp of her bra and pushed the lace aside, she squirmed under his touch, whimpering helplessly as he slowly caressed her, cried out when his mouth closed tightly over one beaded nipple.

She surged upward at the strong pull of his mouth and lips, and the sensation of her fingernails raking over his scalp sent jolts of erotic pleasure dancing over his skin. The last threads of his control stretched taut, and he knew he couldn't wait much longer.

He lifted his head, watched her body writhe under him, thought he might go insane if he didn't have her soon. "Melanie." His hands slid down to her rib cage and tightened. "Open your eyes."

"Hmm?"

His control stretched even tighter when she raised her arms over her head and arched her back. "Open your eyes," he said roughly. "Look at me."

Her eyes slitted open and through the haze of desire, she met his gaze.

His work-roughened hands slid down the satin-smooth skin of her flat belly, skimmed her hips, then caressed the soft inside flesh of her thighs. She quivered under his touch, then inhaled deeply when he slid his fingers under the thin strap of lace covering her silky triangle of dark curls.

She kept her eyes locked with his.

He slipped one finger into the hot, moist folds of

her body, lightly stroked the sensitive skin, watched her twist her hands into the downy softness of the feather bed as she bowed her body upward and rolled her hips.

The last thread of his control snapped.

He needed, desperately needed, to be inside her.

He made a sound in his throat, something deep and guttural, and he yanked the lace down her hips. He moved between her legs and was sheathed deep inside her in one hard thrust. She shuddered at the joining, wrapped her long legs around his waist and took him deeper still. Her hands slid over the tightly bunched muscles of his shoulders and arms, sweat beaded his brow as he moved with an urgency that bordered on madness. She met him thrust for thrust, strained against him, trembled, then cried out as she shuddered fiercely. Her release rippled through him like a shock wave. He rode it to its peak, then, with a deep groan, he toppled off the edge himself.

He collapsed over her, his breathing hoarse and heavy, then rolled to his side and took her with him.

He kissed her cheek, her eyes, her throat.

"Stay," he whispered raggedly. "You and Kevin. Please stay."

He felt her hesitation, heard her slow intake of breath. His chest tightened with dread.

She touched his cheek with her fingertips, then took his face in her hands and looked into his eyes.

"Yes," she said softly. "We'll stay."

Melanie woke slowly, refusing to open her eyes and give up the last, delicious vestiges of sleep. With a sigh, she pulled the warm, fluffy comforter up higher over her exposed shoulder, then turned her cheek and burrowed into the downy softness of the feather bed. She breathed in the masculine scent that lingered there. Gabe's scent. She slid her arm out to reach for him, but felt only cool cotton instead.

That's when the smell of coffee hit her.

Rolling to her back, she stretched languidly. Her body ached in places she didn't know a person could ache, but she was too contented to care. Every inch of her felt absolutely, completely, totally satisfied. Reluctantly she opened her eyes.

The bright sun reflected off the shiny hardwood floor where their clothes were still scattered. Remembering how those clothes got there, she smiled. Remembering what happened afterward, she shivered.

And smiled again.

Curling her fingers into the feather bed, she felt her smile dip as she remembered more than making love. He'd asked her to stay and she'd said yes. The decision terrified as much as it thrilled her.

Her answer had been impulsive, but she'd thought carefully about it in the early-morning hours when Gabe had been sleeping and she'd lain beside him, wide-awake, and simply watched him. She'd left California two months ago, covered her tracks well. She had a new name, Bloomfield County was a small town.

She'd be careful, live a quiet life, maybe even work for the center. No one would question her there. She and Kevin would be as safe here as they would anywhere, she reasoned. Time would be on their side. And at seventy-four, time was something that Louise didn't have as much of as Melanie and Kevin did. The day would come when they would no longer have to look over their shoulder or be afraid of the shadows.

The sound of pans rattling downstairs brought Melanie out of her thoughts. Gabe. She wasn't certain what their future was. He'd never told her that he loved her, but she knew that he cared for her and Kevin very much. He would never hurt them, that she was certain of. For now, that was all she needed. To feel safe.

She knew it was time to tell him the truth.

With a heavy sigh she sat, dragged a hand through her tousled hair, then reached for her wristwatch lying on the floor beside the bed. Good heavens! It was almost ten-thirty. Kevin was supposed to be home soon. If she wanted to talk to Gabe before her son returned, she had better hurry.

She had so much to tell him.

Gabe poured himself a cup of coffee, then went to the refrigerator in search of food. He pulled out eggs, bacon and ham, set them on the counter, then found potatoes and bread and added them to his cache.

He was hungry enough to eat a bear. Two bears.

He'd been grinning like a fool since he'd woken up a little while ago, had even caught himself whistling when he'd measured out the coffee grounds into the basket of the coffeepot.

They weren't leaving. *We'll stay,* she'd said.

He pulled a knife and spatula out of the drawer and set them on the counter, then glanced up at the ceiling when he heard the sound of the upstairs shower running. The image of Melanie naked, her skin glistening and covered with soap brought a sharp tug in his groin. He thought about joining her, not only because he already wanted to make love with her again, but because he simply wanted to hold her, to hear her say it again in the light of day: *We'll stay.*

With Ian and Cara due to bring Kevin back anytime, though, Gabe thought it might not be such a great idea to disturb her shower. They'd have tonight, he thought, and the night after that.

And all the nights after that.

His throat went dry at the significance of that thought. What it meant, where they were headed.

Except he didn't know where they were headed. She said she'd stay, but Lord knew the woman was unpredictable. She could change her mind. One day he might just wake up and she and Kevin would be gone. The thought made his gut twist.

He couldn't live like that. He wouldn't.

No more secrets, he thought darkly. Whatever it was she was running from, whoever it was, Gabe would soon know. Ian should have received the report from Washington last night and he'd bring it with him today. Everything was going to be out in the open. Whatever was in the file, Gabe told himself, he'd deal with it.

He turned at the sound of three short horn blasts. The shower was still running overhead when he walked out onto the front porch. Kevin burst out of the passenger side of the van and raced across the front yard toward him. Sunlight danced in his blond hair; his blue eyes sparkled.

"Gabe! Gabe! I won a prize, I won a prize!"

Gabe held out his arms, and Kevin threw himself into them. He smelled like maple syrup. "It's a twirlybird," Kevin exclaimed. "Wanna see?"

He wiggled away before Gabe could even answer,

held out the bright blue plastic toy and pulled the string. The top spun off with a loud *whizz* and came straight at Gabe. He caught it, and Kevin laughed with delight.

"I wanna show my mom." Kevin snatched the plastic disc from Gabe and started to run toward the front door, then stopped abruptly, ran back and threw his arms around Gabe's legs.

Then he ran back into the house, slamming the wooden screen door behind him.

Stunned, Gabe stood there, staring at the front door. His throat felt as if it were closing up on him, his chest tightened around his heart. And still all he could do was stand there and stare.

"Got to you, hasn't he?"

Gabe turned to look at Ian. "What?"

"He's gotten to you." Ian leaned back against a porch column and grinned. "Kevin and Melanie both. The Sinclair brood are dropping like flies, as the saying goes."

Gabe frowned. He didn't like being compared to a fly, and he sure as hell hadn't "dropped" anywhere yet. The fact that he was well on his way was none of Ian's damn business, Gabe thought irritably. He glanced over at the van, realized that Ian was alone. "Where's Cara?"

"She took one look at all those pancakes this morning, then turned a lovely shade of green and ran out of the room." Ian let out a long, sympathetic sigh. "It passed fast enough, but I took her home anyway before I brought Kevin back. I swear, I was captured once by radicals in Iran and I don't remember feeling that helpless."

Before Gabe had dealt with Kevin being sick, he

might have laughed at Ian. But now, he simply nodded in understanding. When he spotted the manila folder in Ian's hand, he gestured toward it. "Is that for me?"

Frowning, Ian handed Gabe the folder. "You aren't gonna like it."

"I never expected to." The knot in Gabe's stomach tightened as he took the folder.

Ian glanced at the house, then spoke quietly. "Her real name is Melissa Van Camp. She was married to a guy named Phillip Van Camp for five years, until he was killed in a speedboat accident last year. They were living apart at the time."

"She told me about her husband. He was a bastard."

Ian nodded. "Based on the file my resource gathered, a first-class bastard. His father had been a circuit court judge before he died from cancer three years ago, extremely wealthy. Between their money and their connections, it seems that the family considers themselves above the law. Before his death, Phillip had been arrested several times on possession, twice on assault. Oddly enough, every charge was dropped before it even got to trial."

"Who did he assault?" Gabe asked with deadly calm.

"Calm down, Gabe," Ian said quietly. "One incident was a disagreement with a salesclerk, the other was a police officer."

"He hit a cop and got away with it?" Gabe asked in surprise.

"Like I said," Ian went on, "the Van Camps are a prestigious, well-connected family. But considering that Phillip is dead, who he assaulted is not the issue at this point.''

''Then stop pussyfooting around and tell me what is the issue,'' Gabe said impatiently. ''What the hell is Melanie so damn afraid of?''

''Her mother-in-law, for starters.'' Disgust registered on Ian's face. ''Louise Van Camp. According to some reliable resources, after Phillip's death, Louise took over control of Melanie and Kevin's lives, insisted they come live with her, then completely manipulated and dominated them, right down to enrolling Kevin at the same military boarding school that Phillip had gone to. That's when Melanie—Melissa—put her foot down. Or at least she attempted to.''

''What do you mean, 'she attempted to'?''

''She tried to move, start a new life away from Louise in Northern California, but things started happening to her that forced her back under Louise's roof.''

''What kind of things?'' A dark fury twisted Gabe's stomach. He had to force himself to listen, to stay calm.

''A fire in her apartment, her boss at the antique store terminates her for no apparent reason, a male friend from her apartment complex has a mysterious accident and ends up with a broken arm and black eye. And nobody's talking, including Melanie.''

Gabe's single swearword was earthy and to the point. ''That's a hell of a lot of coincidences.''

''So is the fact that before every incident, the same man was seen either with Melanie, or in the area, a man who just happens to work for Louise Van Camp, her so-called 'business manager.' The guy's an ex-con, assault and petty larceny. He's also been a bodyguard, bar bouncer and general all-around slime bucket. His name is Vincent Drake.''

Vincent.

Vincent Drake. Gabe narrowed his eyes, felt his hands close into fists, praying he had an opportunity to meet the guy.

Gabe shook his head in frustration and disbelief. ''Did she ever go to the police with any of this?''

''I went.''

Both men turned sharply at the sound of Melanie's quiet voice from behind the screen door. She stepped out, kept her steely gaze steady on Gabe.

Gabe took a step toward her, stopped at the cold lift of her chin that warned him to stay back. ''Melanie, you have to—''

''I've had enough people tell me what I 'have to,' thank you very much. But I will answer your question. I went to the police once, and for that, a good friend of mine ended up with a broken arm simply for driving me there. If I hadn't dropped the charges, he would have ended up with his other arm broken, as well.''

Her face was pale against the damp waves in her hair, her eyes distant, her voice detached, without emotion. And though he desperately wanted to go to her, he kept his distance, afraid of what she might do if he touched her.

She turned slowly to Ian. ''Would you mind if I spoke to Gabe alone?'' she asked with a cool politeness.

Ian shifted uncomfortably, pressed his lips tightly together as he glanced from her to Gabe. ''I'll be at the tavern.''

Gabe nodded stiffly, watched Ian walk back to his

van and drive away. A warm breeze swept brightly colored leaves onto the front porch. What an odd time, he thought, to realize that the fall leaves had already begun to change.

He dragged a deep breath into his lungs, then slowly released it. "Melanie," he said quietly. "Let us help you. I swear I won't let this guy come anywhere near you."

Her laugh was short and dry. "You just don't get it, do you? You can't stop him. No one can. Anyone who gets too close to me, anyone who tries to help, gets hurt. I can't have that on my conscience. I *won't* have that on my conscience."

"You can't keep running," Gabe said tightly. "What kind of life is that for you and Kevin?"

"A better life than living under Louise's thumb." Her gray eyes darkened to the color of storm clouds. "That military school she wanted Kevin to go to would 'make a man out of him,' she'd said. Teach him to be tough, like his father. Well, if slapping women around is her idea of a man, then she can rot in hell right next to her son when she gets there."

"He hit you?" Gabe's voice was brittle, cold. A fist of rage gripped him, and he struggled to breathe.

"Twice," she said simply. "The first time, I forgave him. He'd had a fight with his mother and he'd been drinking. I just let it go. The second time, I left him. Louise talked me into coming back, told me that he'd been under a lot of stress since his father had died. She promised me that she would talk to him, that it wouldn't happen again. Strangely enough, it didn't, but he continued to have affairs, and there was absolutely nothing between us anymore. I finally filed for divorce, but still Louise refused to see that the marriage was over. She pleaded with me up until the day before Phillip died to drop the divorce."

"Why did you move in with her after Phillip's death?" He shook his head. "Didn't you know what kind of woman she was?"

"She's seventy-four years old, Gabe," Melanie said with quiet patience. "I can't say that she was ever a warm or nice person, but after losing a husband, then a son, something completely snapped in her. Underneath that cold facade of hers, I could see that she was lonely and frightened. But then she started to cling to me and Kevin, demanded to know where we were every second, what we were doing or who we were with. She'd plan our days for us, sulk or manipulate until she got her way."

"Until you gave in." Gabe heard the irritation in his own voice. Her gaze snapped up sharply.

"Don't judge me, Gabe," she said tightly. "You have no right. You weren't there. You don't know what it was like, what she was like. I thought I was helping her."

He nodded, felt ashamed that he'd turned his frustration on her. "You're right," he said quietly. "I'm sorry."

She drew in a slow, deep breath, and her shoulders relaxed a bit. "She's my son's grandmother. Kevin is all that Louise has left. I guess I felt sorry for her. On top of that, after Phillip died, I discovered that almost everything we owned was in Louise's name. When I lost my manager position at the antique store, Kevin and I needed a place to stay while I was looking for a new job. I had no idea that Louise was responsible not only for me losing my job, but for preventing me from finding a new one. By the time I found out, it was too late.''

Gabe's eyes narrowed. ''What do you mean, it was 'too late'?''

She folded her arms tightly around her, then stared blankly into a distant stand of maples. The sun was directly overhead in a blue, cloudless sky, and a hawk soared over the open meadow. Melanie watched the hawk circle soundlessly, then suddenly dive down, its claws extended as it skimmed the ground. Gabe saw her wince at the sight, then she slowly turned her attention back to him.

''Vincent.'' Her hand skimmed the base of her throat. ''Vincent Drake.''

Once again, Gabe felt his insides twist coldly at the name. ''Who is he?'' Gabe asked quietly. ''What did he do to you?''

''Originally Louise hired the man as a driver and bodyguard, but then she starting calling him her 'business manager.' Suddenly the man was everywhere Kevin and I were, always watching us. He gave me the creeps. When I complained, Louise told me she was worried about kidnapping, and that Vincent's protection was for mine and Kevin's own good. I moved out after that. Vincent 'convinced' me to come back.''

''You mean he threatened you,'' Gabe said with barely controlled rage.

She nodded. ''His threats were subtle in the beginning, but I got the picture. When I took a second stand against Louise and moved to Northern California, he found me. This time he wasn't subtle. My apartment caught on fire, then Paul, a friend I'd made at my apartment house suddenly had a broken arm, simply because he'd driven me to the police station to file a complaint. When Vincent threatened to break Paul's other arm, I had no choice but to go back again."

Gabe's hand tightened on the folder he held. He looked forward to meeting Vincent Drake. He only hoped it would be soon. Very soon.

He drew in a slow breath to steady himself. "Go on."

"I was afraid to go to the police again," she said so quietly that Gabe could barely hear her. "Afraid who Vincent might hurt if I did. I secretly tried to hire a lawyer to help me. Louise found out and she was furious, told me I was ungrateful for all she'd done for me and Kevin. The lawyer never returned my calls after that. Louise began telling people that I was having some kind of a breakdown, that I was mentally unstable. I was terrified that she was going to take Kevin away from me. With her connections, with all her money, she would probably win. I couldn't risk that."

"So you ran."

"I bought a car with cash, found someone who manufactured a phony ID for me, took what little money I'd managed to save and left in the middle of the night. I was going to my friend Raina's, in Boston, but she told me someone was watching her. I didn't think they knew about her, but somehow they found out and it wasn't safe anymore."

Melanie pressed her lips into a hard, thin line. "If Vincent finds me and Kevin, he'll make us go back. That's why I kept moving, never stayed in one place until I came here, why I wanted to keep moving."

"I won't let him near you or Kevin." Gabe's hands

fisted at his sides. "If he shows up here, I swear to you he'll be one sorry bastard."

With a heavy sigh, she shook her head. "You can't always be here, Gabe. And what about Cara? Or Abby? Or your brothers? Vincent likes to inflict pain, he enjoys it. How could I live with myself if any one of you were hurt because of me?"

"We take care of our own. All of us. Louise isn't the only one with connections. Ian has a few himself. He could look into this, make sure that—"

"Wait." Her head snapped up, and her eyes opened wide as she stared at the file in Gabe's hand. "How did Ian know who I really am? Oh my God," she gasped. "What have you done?"

"You were ready to bolt any minute," he said tightly. "Ian has resources, so I asked him to run a check on you."

"You had no right!" Her voice rose, her eyes flashed. "No right at all!"

"I *took* the right, dammit!" He was yelling now and he didn't even care. "I couldn't, *wouldn't,* stand around and do nothing, then watch you and Kevin walk out of my life. I care about you, both of you. Whether you like it or not, I'm going to help you."

She shook her head fiercely. "If your investigation alerts even one of Louise's connections, Vincent will find me here. I can't let that happen. I can't!"

She turned and headed for the front door, but he moved in front of her and blocked her way. "What are you going to do?"

"Get out of my way." Her chin lifted defiantly.

He shook his head. "Not until you tell me what you're going to do."

"I was going to stay," she said with a chilly calm.

"I was coming down here to tell you everything, tell you I was going to risk everything just to be here with you. Now that you've done this, now that Vincent might find me, I don't know what I'm going to do."

"Melanie—"

"I need to be alone, Gabe." Hurt darkened her gray eyes. "I need you to go into town and leave me alone so I can think."

He wanted to shake her, wanted to pull her into his arms and hold her, but he knew he couldn't touch her, that she didn't want him near her right now.

Maybe it would do them both good for him to leave her alone for a little while. He could take his frustration out on his brothers and she'd have time to calm down, to realize that he'd only done what he had to do.

"You go ahead and think." He stepped out of the way. "But I'll be back, Melanie. You can count on it."

Her gaze met his for the briefest moment, but he couldn't read what was going on inside her. She moved past him, and the screen door closed behind her.

Dammit! He spun on his heels and headed for his truck.

Chapter 12

Melanie stood at the upstairs bedroom window and stared across the long expanse of lush meadow that had been Mildred Witherspoon's front yard. Thick stands of dogwoods and maples surrounded the property, the lush green leaves already changing. Another week or two and she imagined the entire countryside would be a beautiful patchwork of rich reds and browns, golden-yellows and brilliant orange.

But would she be here to see it?

Turning from the window, she stared at the open suitcase on the floor behind her. She'd started to pack, certain that she couldn't stay, couldn't take the chance that Ian's inquiries into her life would expose her and Kevin to danger. Panicked, she'd tossed half of her clothes into the suitcase when she'd glanced at the feather bed on the floor and remembered the night before. Remembered how safe and warm she'd felt in Gabe's arms. How protected and loved.

Only to find out that he'd gone behind her back, run his own investigation and delved into matters he didn't understand, that he couldn't possibly understand.

He had no right, dammit! she'd told herself over and over as she'd paced the bedroom. No right. It was her life, hers and Kevin's. When she'd left California, she'd vowed that no one would take control of her life again. She would make her own decisions, do what *she* thought was best for her and her son.

She closed her eyes, listened to Kevin's laughter as he played with his twirlybird downstairs. He was so happy here. Happier than he'd ever been. Bloomfield County was a wonderful town, exactly the kind of place she'd want to raise her son.

To raise a family.

Melanie hadn't let herself even consider the possibility of more children, not with the life she and Kevin faced. Always looking over their shoulders, wondering if Vincent might find them.

But still, ever since Cara's announcement last night, she'd felt a yearning, a desperate longing that had slipped in under her defenses and whispered seductively in her ear. A brother for Kevin, a little girl for her.

A dark-haired little boy. A green-eyed baby girl. Gabe's hair, Gabe's eyes.

Melanie's chest ached.

Gabe had told her before that he hadn't wanted to raise another family, that raising his brothers and Cara had been enough for him. She knew he cared for her, that he wanted to help her, but was it just his instinctive protective nature to help a woman in trouble, or was it more? There was a strong physical bond between them, but he'd said nothing about love, certainly nothing about marriage.

Was she a fool to hope?

But even more immediate, was he right about her staying here? Was it time to stop running? Was it possible that here, with Gabe, and the support of the Sinclairs and Shawnessys, that she and Kevin might have a future? A future that included Gabe?

She desperately wanted to believe that, but they didn't know Vincent, didn't know what the man was capable of doing to them.

Her head hurt. She'd been so certain of what she had to do, so absolutely positive. And now the indecision was clawing at her insides, shredding away her confidence. She didn't know anymore. She simply didn't know.

With a heavy sigh, she rubbed her throbbing temple, then started downstairs to find her son. Maybe just looking at him, or holding him in her arms would help her decide.

Her footsteps echoed in the empty house as she made her way down the stairs. She'd miss this house, with its smooth oak hardwood floors, high beveled ceilings and open sunny kitchen. Her fingers slid over the polished oak banister. She could picture pine garland draped over the railing, decorated with big red holiday bows. She could even smell a turkey roasting, hear the sounds of caroling as snow fell silently outside.

Dreaming of snowmen and sleigh rides, she walked into the kitchen in search of her son.

That's when the dream ended and the nightmare began.

Vincent Drake sat at the kitchen table holding Kevin on his lap.

"You gonna drink that beer, or just stare it down with that ugly scowl on your face until it jumps in your mouth?"

Gabe turned the ugly scowl Reese was referring to on his brother. "If you're counting on tips for your clever wit, little brother, you're gonna starve to death."

"Everyone knows Reese flunked the Tavern Keeper's School of Comedy," Callan chimed in, keeping his eyes locked on the ball game on the overhead television. "Bring your infield closer, Johnson, he's gonna bunt. There he goes!" Callan slapped the counter and coffee sloshed out of the cup in his hands. "Told you!"

Reese grabbed a fluffy white bar towel and wiped the glossy oak countertop until it shone. "I'm gonna starve to death just giving my brothers' free beer and coffee. And I sure as hell would starve if I counted on you all for tips."

"Didn't I tell you not to date Julie Hecker? That's one hell of a tip, if you ask me." Lucian was working on his second cup of strong, black coffee and his eyes were just beginning to clear. "Besides, you wiped me out last night with that damn straight flush. You are one lucky bastard."

"That's what all the women say." Callan sipped his coffee. "Only without the lucky part."

"Sydney Taylor would agree with that," Lucian said dryly. "She flew in here last night spitting nails 'cause Boomer was digging in her vegetable garden.

Said if Reese didn't keep that mutt of his locked up, she'd tie him up and put a muzzle on him."

"Reese?" Ian asked when he came back from using the phone in Reese's office. "Or the dog?"

"That would probably be the only way Sydney could get a man." Lucian reached for a slice of orange that Reese was cutting up. "She's not hard to look at, but she could sculpt ice with that tongue of hers. It oughta get real interesting around here when she opens that fancy French restaurant across the street."

"I can handle Sydney." Reese took a bite of orange and wiggled his brows. "But can she handle me?"

Shaking his head at their foolishness, Gabe glanced at his watch for what had to be the tenth time already since he'd sat down. He'd told himself he would give Melanie an hour alone to think. Only twenty minutes had passed. His hand tightened on the beer he had yet to even taste.

"Looks like Reese isn't the only one with female problems," Lucian said with a grin. "What's the matter, bro? Did Melanie send you packing?"

Lucian's comment hit a little too close for comfort. Gabe made a rude comment to Lucian, which only raised eyebrows and garnered attention all around.

"Someone's after her, dammit," he blurted out suddenly, though he hadn't meant to. "Some slime named Vincent Drake who enjoys hurting people and scaring children. I may have made it possible for him to find her."

His brothers all went still. Their grins slowly faded. Gabe glanced at Ian, who shrugged, then said,

"They'll know soon enough. You might as well tell them everything."

He took a deep breath and then he did, starting with everything that Ian's investigation had turned up, plus what Melanie had told him. By the time he'd finished, Lucian, Reese and Callan all stood stiff and grim, their expressions dark and fierce.

"Just let that bastard take one step in this town," Lucian said with deadly calm. "No one messes with a Sinclair woman."

A Sinclair woman. That's exactly what Melanie was, Gabe decided. A Sinclair woman.

His woman.

He'd never felt this way toward any woman before, never felt this fierce, savage need to protect, to take care of. Not just for the moment, not just for next week, but forever. The realization hit him like a lumberjack's fist.

He didn't just care about her, and it sure as hell wasn't just sex. He loved her. Her and Kevin both.

"You okay?" Reese leaned over the counter and waved a hand in front of his face.

"Yeah, sure." He scrubbed a hand over his bristled face. "Fine."

"Afternoon, boys." Cherry Barnes set three plates of mile-high turkey sandwiches and hot French fries on the bar. Cherry, a perky redhead with a showgirl's body, had been working extra hours on the weekends for Reese, trying to save enough money so she could head for the bright lights of Vegas. "Hey, you talkin' about that pretty brunette staying out at the Witherspoon house? The one with the cute little blond kid that Gabe brought here last week? What a coincidence!"

Cherry suddenly had the attention of every male surrounding her, a fact that she dearly loved.

"Why is it a coincidence?" Gabe asked carefully.

"Well," Cherry breathed excitedly, "her brother was in here earlier for some breakfast and coffee, said that he was on his way out to see her and her kid, but he'd gotten a little lost and needed directions."

With a rough oath, Gabe flew off his seat, knocking the bar stool onto the floor. Cherry squeaked, then jumped out of the way as the five men moved as a solid unit toward the exit.

"We'll take the van," Ian said tightly. "We can work up a plan on the way there. We can be there in ten minutes."

"I'm going to take my truck and come up from behind the house." Gabe looked at Ian. "Have you got a gun?"

Ian yanked his keys out of his pocket, then unlocked a hidden compartment under the driver's seat. Even though Ian no longer worked for the government, a man never knew when his past might tap him on the shoulder. He pulled out a .22 and handed it to Gabe.

"Don't let him see your van." Gabe took the gun, checked the safety, then shoved it into the waistband of his jeans. He looked at Ian and his brothers. "If one of you finds him first, save him for me. Vincent Drake is mine," Gabe said fiercely, then jumped into his truck and spun gravel from the rear wheels as he roared off.

Dammit, dammit, *dammit!* He never should have left her alone, no matter what she'd said or wanted.

Hang on, Melanie, he said over and over as he turned the next corner on two wheels. If anything happened to her or Kevin, Gabe knew he couldn't bear it.

Vincent Drake was a dead man.

Cold terror settled over Melanie as she stared at Vincent holding her son.

No, no, no! she screamed silently, but her throat had closed up and simply refused to work.

Dressed in a black T-shirt, black blazer and slacks, Vincent looked like the devil himself.

"Mommy!" Kevin tried to jump off Vincent's lap, but the man's beefy arms held him still.

"Hey, we're buddies, remember?" Vincent hugged Kevin tighter and stroked the top of his head. "Didn't I promise you a new video game when we go back home?"

"I don't wanna go back!" Kevin jerked his head away, then thrust his lower lip out in an angry pout. "I like it here."

Melanie choked back a sob, watched helplessly as Vincent continued to stroke the top of her son's head.

"Don't!" Melanie managed to find her voice somehow, though even the single word felt like sandpaper in her throat. "Don't you touch him."

"Melissa, Melissa." Vincent sighed heavily, shook his head at her as if she were a recalcitrant child. "Is that any way to speak to an old friend?"

"You are not my friend," she snarled through her teeth, praying that her knees wouldn't give out on her.

"Of course I am." Vincent smiled, and the evil in his black eyes closed over her like a spiderweb. "And soon, Melissa, my dear, we are going to be the very best of friends. Close, *intimate* friends."

Oh dear Lord. Her blood turned to ice at his threat.

He would punish her that way, she knew he would. He'd always looked at her that way, but she knew he'd never gone that far before because Louise had never given permission. But he wouldn't ask permission this time. He was out of control, angry. She could see it in his eyes. And he'd make her pay.

She couldn't think about that, she couldn't. If she did, she'd never find the strength to fight him.

And she would fight him. This time, she would fight him with everything she had. She'd made that decision before he'd even found her, though she hadn't realized it until this very minute. She wouldn't run anymore, wouldn't live her life always looking over her shoulder, wondering when the devil would be knocking at her door.

He was knocking now, Melanie knew, and she would face him down.

No matter what it took, no matter what she had to do, this time she would not give in. She'd be strong not only for herself and for her son, but for Gabe. Her love for him made her stronger than she'd ever been before.

"How did you find us?" she managed to ask, and was surprised that her voice wasn't shaking like her insides.

"I will say that you certainly made it interesting this time." He gave an amused chuckle, then his smile slowly faded. "I was too easy on you before, Melissa. I'm afraid you didn't take me seriously. This time you will, believe me."

"But how did you find us?" she asked again. If nothing else, Melanie thought, she would buy time, try to keep him talking. Maybe, just maybe, Gabe would come back, though the thought that he would return also terrified her. How could she live with herself if Vincent hurt Gabe?

Vincent frowned with impatience. "Well, now, I can't exactly go around giving away my secrets, now can I? Let's just say that the right amount of money to the right people gets the job done. It cost me big time, Melissa," he said, narrowing his eyes. "And I'm afraid it's going to cost you, too. You have five minutes to get your things together. There's a plane waiting for us at the airport."

She'd have to do this herself, she realized. Somehow she'd fight this man, and she would win. She had to.

"You need to leave." Where it came from she didn't know, but even with the fear pounding in her temples, Melanie found the strength to defy him. "I'm not alone anymore, Vincent. I have friends here. They won't let you take me and Kevin back."

"Ah, yes, your friends." Vincent nodded slowly. "You know, it simply amazes me how friendly the people in small towns are, how talkative. I know all about your 'friends,' Melissa, dear. You and this fellow—what's his name—Gabe Sinclair? According to a cute little redhead over at the tavern in town, well, you two are quite close. I wouldn't normally believe gossip like that, but I saw him come out of here this morning and sure enough, the rumor appears to be true."

Vincent's left eye twitched, and his smile was cold. "I also heard that his sister has been quite helpful to you, and that she's expecting her first child. Such a delicate time for a woman, isn't it?"

Melanie's heart stopped, then slammed against her ribs. He would do something horrible like that, she thought wildly. Hurt Cara or anyone else who got in his way.

Black fury twisted Melanie's stomach. Never before had she wished someone dead, not even when Vincent had hurt Paul, then forced her to come back to Louise. But she wished that now for Vincent, wished him to hell for all he'd done.

Her anger gave her a strength she didn't know she had. Vincent didn't know the Sinclairs and the Shawnessys, what they were like, how strong they were, how united. Vincent thought he was untouchable, but he was far from it. If he threatened Cara, touched one hair on her head, justice would be swift and hard, without mercy.

And somehow, in her heart, she knew that they would do the same for her and Kevin. They'd taken her into their family, and they would take care of her and her son as they would one of their own.

And then, sitting next to all the food that Gabe had taken out earlier, Melanie spotted the knife.

Her gaze flicked back to Vincent, and a steady calm came over her, a quiet knowledge that he wouldn't win this time. She smiled, was amazed that her legs managed to take her across the kitchen until she stood beside him, was even more amazed that she was able to touch him without wincing.

She slid her fingers up his arm, felt the solid muscle of his shoulders. He was stronger than her, bigger than her, but it didn't matter. She wasn't afraid of him anymore, refused to let this coward ever intimidate her again.

Surprised by Melanie's abrupt change, Vincent didn't even try to stop Kevin when he reached for his mother. Calmly she took her son in her arms, then set him down on the floor.

"Kevin, you take your twirlybird and go play outside while I talk to Vincent." Melanie kept her gaze on the man, prayed that the look she gave him was as seductive as she meant it to be. "I'll come get you in a little while."

Kevin narrowed his eyes at Vincent, then looked back at his mother with uncertainty.

"It's all right, sweetie." Melanie smoothed a hand over her son's head. "We won't be long."

Kevin snatched his toy off the table, gave Vincent another furious look, then ran out the back door. She gave a silent prayer of thanks that he'd minded her, then turned her attention back to Vincent. The expression in his eyes was wary, but she saw the interest there as well. What she knew she had to do repulsed her, but she would do anything to protect her son and gain back the life that she rightfully deserved.

"I'm actually glad you found us, you know." She ran her fingers over Vincent's scalp, and the slick, oily feel of his hair made bile rise in her throat. "It all seemed like such a grand game, me disappearing, then you pursuing. Always the anticipation, wondering if this would be the day you would find us."

He narrowed his eyes suspiciously, but she could see she had his attention. Leaning in close, she whispered breathlessly in his ear. "It excites me, Vincent. Living with Phillip, then Louise, life couldn't get much more boring than that. And then you came along, a handsome, strong man—" she struggled not to choke "—and I saw the chance for a little fun, some thrills."

The lust in his eyes darkened, but the suspicion was

ll there. He grabbed hold of her wrist and jerked it ughly behind her back, bringing her body closer to s. "You really think I'm stupid enough to believe at?"

She could hardly answer that question truthfully. ough every instinct in her screamed to move away om him, she leaned against him and smiled. "I'm k of being at Louise's beck and call, just like you ust be. You're not a yes-man, Vincent. You're not e kind of man who lets a woman tell him what to . I admire that kind of strength in a man."

He hadn't released her, but his grip loosened. "I n sick of that old broad telling me what to do. But e pays me enough to take it for now." With his e hand he reached up and grabbed her breast. What have you got to offer?"

She bit the inside of her mouth to distract herself om the repulsion coursing through her. She arched to him, as if she enjoyed his groping, disgusting uch.

"I hoarded close to a half million dollars away in l the years I was married to Phillip. The Van Camps e so rich, and so stupid, they never even noticed. 'e don't have to go back. You and me and Kevin, e can all just disappear. You're smart enough to do at. I've just been waiting for you to find me. I'm ed of this hick town. Let's go to New York or Chi- go. Have a good time." She pulled her wrist from s hold and moved behind him, sliding her hands ver his shoulders, then said huskily, "A real good me."

He stood suddenly, turned and reached for her. miling, she jumped back and put up a hand for him stop while she reached for the top buttons on her

blouse. His gaze fell greedily on her exposed skin
he advanced. She forced a giggle, still unbuttoni
her blouse, praying that he'd keep his attention on h
breasts.

She backed against the kitchen counter, had thr
buttons open when she reached behind her a
grabbed the knife lying there and swung it around
front of her.

Vincent froze, then smiled slowly. "I knew y
were up to something, you little bitch. But it doesn
matter. We'll have a little 'fun' here, just like y
wanted. Only I think the fun's going to be all mine
He moved closer, his lips curling into a sneer. "I
you really think that little knife is going to stop me

She waved the knife furiously, watching as his ey
followed the blade. "Actually, no," she said evenl
"But I think *this* will."

She kicked out furiously, glad that she was weari
heavy boots. She made a hard, direct connection wi
his groin, and he crumpled like an aluminum can.

She didn't stop to look, she ran out the back do

When she burst out onto the back porch, she sa
Kevin playing by the big oak beside the garage.

"Run, Kevin!" she screamed. "Run!"

He glanced up, and she saw the fear in his eye
then the terror as Vincent stumbled out the back do
after her, doubled over.

Kevin spun and ran toward the cornfields, then di
appeared into the tall stalks. Relief poured throu
her. She turned to face Vincent, to hold him back
long as she could and give her son time to run a
hide.

But she turned too slow, and as she came aroun
Vincent's fist caught her on the jaw. Stars explod

ıd pain shot through her head. She went down into ..e soft dirt, felt the crisp press of fall leaves on her ıeek, smelled the thick scent of damp earth. Tasted ıe tangy warmth of blood in her mouth. Her arms ıd legs refused to move, though she screamed si-ntly at her body to get up, to stop Vincent.

"Run, baby, run," she whispered again, though she new her son couldn't hear her.

Gabe flew down the dirt access road beside the ornfield, then plunged directly into the field when ıe roof of the Witherspoon house came into view. Ie knew he couldn't drive all the way up to the ouse; if Vincent Drake had found Melanie, then abe knew his arrival would put both her and Kevin ı danger.

He drove another fifty yards into the center of the eld, plowing through the rows of corn, then slammed n his brakes and jumped out of the cab.

His feet had barely hit the ground when he heard Ielanie scream for Kevin to run. He heard the panic ı her voice, and the sound turned his blood to ice. Ie started for the house, his heart hammering in his hest as he lunged through the cornstalks, then froze t the sound of thrashing no more than ten yards from im.

"You let go of me!"

At the sound of Kevin's sharp cry, Gabe's heart topped. Jaw clenched tight, he pulled the gun from he waistband of his jeans and silently slid through he stalks of corn. His breath came in short gasps as ıe followed the sound of Kevin's furious protests.

He came up behind them, saw Kevin struggling to scape the man's hold on his arms. The sight of the

guy manhandling the little boy made Gabe blind wi
rage. His fingers tightened on the cold steel in h
hands as he lifted the gun.

"Let go of him," Gabe demanded harsh
"Now."

Still holding onto Kevin's arms, Vincent spun
the sound of Gabe's command. As he spotted the gu
his eyes widened, then he snatched Kevin closer
him.

"Gabe!" Dust rose around Kevin's boots as
tried to wiggle free, but Vincent only tightened h
hold.

"Well, well, if it isn't one of Melissa's *friends.*
Vincent smiled thinly. "She's told me so much abo
you."

"She's told me all about you, too. You're a v
cious, cowardly bastard who likes to terrorize wom
and children." Gabe gestured with the gun. "Now l
the boy go."

"Dear me, such compliments. My heart's all aflu
ter." Vincent's smile widened, and he dragged Kev
closer still. "Well now, if Melissa, or *Melanie,* as yc
know her, has indeed told you all about me, then yc
know you better put that gun down before I give yc
a demonstration of my more admirable traits."

Kevin cried out when Vincent tightly grabbed h
shoulders. *Dammit!* Gabe knew the bastard would c
whatever he needed to do to take Kevin and Melani
even if it meant hurting a little boy.

At the sudden movement beside him, Gabe turne
sharply, then saw Melanie appear, her eyes wide wi
terror. Gabe swore silently at the sight of her red ja
and open blouse. His rage turned murderous, and h

knew that before this was over Vincent Drake would pay dearly for all he'd done to Kevin and Melanie.

"Gabe," Melanie whispered hoarsely. "Do as he says. Please."

Clenching his jaw, Gabe turned back to Vincent, narrowing his eyes as he tossed the gun aside.

"I don't need a gun to take care of you," Gabe said calmly, then glanced down at Kevin. "In fact, I don't need anything to handle a scumbag like you. Even Kevin could take you down, you overblown bag of dirt, can't you, Kevin?"

Vincent started to laugh, but as Kevin's eyes met Gabe's, they both understood what it was that he needed to do.

Kevin pressed his lips tightly together, concentrated hard, then looked down. Vincent didn't even see it coming when the heel of Kevin's boot came down solidly on the arch of his foot. Vincent howled at the pain, and startled, let go of Kevin.

Kevin ran to Gabe, but he pushed him toward his mother. "Get back to the house. Ian and my brothers are there." When she hesitated, he yelled, "Now, dammit!"

Melanie snatched Kevin up in her arms and ran.

Gabe turned back to Vincent as the man reared up. With a roar, Gabe charged.

They both flew into the cornstalks and went down, fists flying. Gabe brought his arm back and swung, connecting with Vincent's nose. He bellowed in pain, then swung his own meaty fist and caught Gabe in the jaw, sending him backward.

Gabe rolled, then sprang to his feet, arms stretched out wide. "Come on," he jeered, wiggling his fingers.

"Let's see how you do when you're face-to-face with a man."

Hatred glistened in Vincent's eyes as he lifted his head. Blood spurted from his nose. With a shout, Vincent came at him.

Gabe welcomed the attack, and landed a solid, powerful fist in Vincent's soft gut. The air whooshed out of his lungs, and he went down on his knees. Gabe slammed a fist into the man's jaw, which sent him flying backward. Vincent's head lolled to one side as Gabe grabbed him by his jacket and raised him up. He hit him again and this time, Vincent went down, limp and lifeless.

Gabe was reaching for him again, had his arm already poised to strike when Lucian came up behind him and said quietly, "Gabe, he's out. It's over."

Gabe blinked several times, stared at Vincent's battered face, then shoved the man back to the ground. Vincent didn't move.

"He's still breathing," Gabe said through clenched teeth, then looked at his brother. "You have Melanie and Kevin?"

"We have them." Lucian put a hand on Gabe's shoulder. "You all right?"

Gabe nodded slowly. "I'll be better when this slimeball is behind bars."

"The sheriff is on his way." Lucian glanced down at Vincent. "We'll need to take him back up to the house."

Lucian smiled, and Gabe felt just a little of the tension ease.

They each grabbed a leg and pulled.

Melanie watched Gabe step out onto the front porch, his face bloodied, his shirt torn and dirty. Her knees nearly crumpled at the sight of him, and she hugged her son tightly to her to give her strength.

She'd hoped, prayed, that he would have come to her right away, but he'd come back more than twenty minutes ago from the cornfield with Lucian, both of them dragging a moaning Vincent. Twenty minutes had felt like a lifetime. She desperately wanted to run to him now, but she knew her legs wouldn't make it, wasn't certain that he would even want her. She'd sent him away, hadn't trusted him, and she knew how much that had hurt him.

Callan stood beside her; he'd brought her out here on the porch, away from all the chaos in the kitchen where Gabe and Lucian had dragged Vincent and tied him in a chair. Callan and Reese had found her stumbling out of the cornfield earlier with her son in her arms. Callan had gently taken Kevin from her, then Reese had simply scooped her up in his arms and carried her into the house. Lucian had already gone into the fields to help Gabe, and Ian hadn't been far behind. Sirens screaming, the sheriff and his deputy had arrived ten minutes ago and were busy taking statements inside.

Gabe's eyes were intense as he stared at her now, his brow furrowed. When Kevin caught sight of Gabe, he pulled away from his mother and ran to him, threw his little arms around Gabe's legs. Melanie couldn't stop the tears sliding down her cheeks.

Gabe picked Kevin up and held him fiercely to him. "You okay, partner?"

Kevin nodded. "I did what you taught me, Gabe. I stomped on his foot real hard and made him let me go."

"You were great." Gabe smiled at Kevin. "Even Batman couldn't have done a better job."

Kevin beamed at that. "Will that bad man go away now and leave us alone?"

"He won't ever bother you or your mommy again. He's going to go to jail for a very long time." Gabe looked at Melanie, his expression grim. "Based on the way Vincent is spilling his guts in there, thanks to Ian's persuasive questioning skills, Louise may be spending some time behind bars, as well. Even her money and connections won't get her out of this one."

In spite of everything, Melanie felt a twinge of sorrow for the woman. Louise may have brought this on herself, but in her own twisted way, she had loved Kevin, just as she'd loved Phillip. She was an old woman who would never know her grandson, and for that, Melanie was truly sorry.

Melanie watched as Kevin wrapped his arms around Gabe's neck and hugged him. She wanted so badly to do the same, but she still wasn't certain what he was feeling right now, what he was thinking. She only knew she couldn't bear it if, after everything they'd been through, he turned away from her now.

"Would you like to go show Callan how your twirly-bird flies?" Gabe pulled the toy out of his back pocket. "If it's okay with you, I'd like to talk to your mommy for a little bit."

Kevin hesitated, but when Callan held out his hand, the boy smiled and snatched up the toy, then took Callan's hand and pulled him out into the front yard.

Her throat thick with tears, her chest tight with a mixture of hope and dread, Melanie clasped her hands in front of her and faced Gabe.

He still hadn't moved toward her, hadn't touched her. And she needed him to, so much that she ached.

She smiled, but she felt the trembling in her lips. "Thank you."

His mouth thinned. "You don't have to thank me, Melanie. Or should I call you Melissa now?"

Her heart sank. He *was* angry, very angry, she thought, based on the tight set of his jaw. How could she blame him? After everything he'd done for her, and the way she'd treated him?

"I prefer Melanie," she said softly. "That's who I am now. And I do have to thank you. You've given me and my son back our lives."

Her words tightened the knot of fear already twisting Gabe's gut. She could leave now, he realized. Go back to her old life, her old job that she'd loved so much. Have all the things she'd left behind in California.

"And what does that mean?" Gabe asked carefully.

Her brow wrinkled with confusion. "What does what mean?"

The adrenaline was still pumping through his veins, and he knew he needed to keep his distance or he might frighten her with the raw need he felt for her right now. He wanted to crush her against him, bury his face in her neck, feel the beat of her heart against his.

"What does it mean?" he asked impatiently. "What will you do now?"

Her gaze flicked up anxiously to his; her hand curled into a fist on her chest. "What should I do?"

He shook his head. "You tell me, Melanie. This time, you have to tell me."

Her soft gray eyes sharpened, then she lifted her chin and said firmly, "I want to stay in Bloomfield County, Gabe. With you, if you still want me."

Relief poured through him, almost brought him to his knees. Slowly, carefully, he moved toward her, gently took her in his arms and held her against him. "If I want you?" he said hoarsely. "Good Lord, woman, are you completely blind? I want you so much it hurts."

She sagged against him, and he felt the warm dampness of her tears through his shirt. Tenderly he brushed her hair back with his fingertips, let her have her cry, though every sob ripped through him like a knife.

After a few minutes, he pulled back, wiped her tears away with the pad of his thumb, then tilted her chin up and frowned. The red welt on her jaw turned his gut inside out, and he struggled to tamp down the rage that threatened to explode once again. He'd deal with that emotion later, he told himself. Work out his frustration on a punching bag in the weight room at Sam's gym in town.

"I love you," he whispered, and though he'd never said the words to any woman before, they felt right. "Marry me. You and Kevin. Please marry me."

There were fresh tears in her eyes now, he prayed they were tears of joy. When she laughed suddenly, then threw her arms around his neck, he released the breath he'd been holding.

"Oh, yes, yes, I will, we will. Oh, Gabe, I love you, too."

He held her for a long moment, too overcome to speak, then eased away from her and looked into her eyes. "Vincent told the sheriff he bribed someone in the phone company to run a trace on area codes until they found a match with Raina's phone number. There was a record of the call you'd made from my cell phone, the one I overheard upstairs. That call led him here."

He squeezed his eyes shut, pulled her tightly to him again. "Oh, baby," he whispered, "I'm so sorry I didn't get here sooner. I died a thousand deaths on the drive over here, knowing that he'd tracked you down and you were here all alone."

She put her finger to his lips, shook her head. "No, Gabe, it's me who should be sorry. I was afraid to trust you, even though I knew I loved you, I was still afraid. I know now that you didn't want to control me or take over my life, you just wanted to help me, to take care of me and Kevin. I let Phillip and Louise blind me to what real love is, which is trust and sharing and respect. Can you ever forgive me?"

He smiled, answered her by drawing her close for a long, tender kiss. They were both breathing heavily by the time he pulled away.

"There is still one little question," he said softly, brushing his lips with hers.

"What?" She curled her fingers into the front of his shirt.

"Where we'll live."

"Anywhere," she murmured, pressed her lips to his neck.

"I know a great place for sale." He ever-so-gently touched his mouth to the red spot on her jaw. "But it has a lot of bedrooms, so we'd have to have a lot of kids to fill them."

She pulled away from him, her eyes bright with

moisture. "Oh, Gabe," she breathed. "Do you mean, do you think.... Oh, *Gabe!*"

He caught her as she jumped into his arms and smothered his face with kisses. Kevin ran up then to see what all the commotion was about and Callan watched, a big grin on his face, as Gabe scooped Kevin up and swung both the boy and his mother off their feet.

At the sound of horns honking, they turned and watched as both Cara and Abby approached the house in their cars.

His family was all here, Gabe thought as he set Melanie back on her feet. He slipped an arm around her waist, then placed a hand on Kevin's shoulder.

All of his family.

* * * * *

There will be more stories
of the Sinclair Brothers
in Silhouette Desire.

Look for their romances in 2001.